MW00623015

MISLAID
IN PARTS
HALF-KNOWN

MISLAID
IN PARTS
HALF-KNOWN

SEANAN
McGUIRE

TOR DOT COM

TOR PUBLISHING GROUP

NEW YORK

MISLAID IN PARTS HALF-KNOWN

Copyright © 2023 by Seanan McGuire

Interior illustrations by Rovina Cai

A Tordotcom Book
Published by Tom Doherty Associates / Tor Publishing Group
120 Broadway
New York, NY 10271

www.tor.com

Tor® is a registered trademark of Macmillan Publishing Group, LLC.

The Library of Congress Cataloging-in-Publication Data
is available upon request.

ISBN 978-1-250-84850-5 (hardback)
ISBN 978-1-250-84851-2 (ebook)

Our books may be purchased in bulk for promotional,
educational, or business use. Please contact your local bookseller
or the Macmillan Corporate and Premium Sales Department
at 1-800-221-7945, extension 5442, or by email at
MacmillanSpecialMarkets@macmillan.com.

First Edition: 2024

Printed in the United States of America

0 9 8 7 6 5 4 3 2

FOR KATHLEEN AND BAXTER.

IN A WORLD FULL OF LOST THINGS,
THANK YOU FOR HELPING ME FIND MY HEART AGAIN.

I'm a friend to the desperate and daunted
Companion to beggars and kings, I do not
Envy the thrones of the mighty, I am content
As the god of lost things.

Only don't ask me for hope or for innocence
Keep this in mind as you pray
I am the god of lost things but I cannot comfort you.

—"The God of Lost Things," Talis Kimberley

PART I

SOMETIMES THINGS GET FOUND

LOST AND FOUND

CHILDREN OF THE DOORS know about being mislaid. They are well-acquainted with stepping through an opening or following a passage that should lead from *here* to *there,* and finding themselves someplace entirely else, someplace entirely new. It is possibly their only truly unifying experience, the one thing they have so completely in common that there's no need to even question it: once upon a time, they took an impossible step, opened an impossible portal, and ended up in a terribly, horribly possible place.

It's inevitable that some worlds have known more than one traveler, but the majority of the wandering children went to totally different places, to worlds so dissimilar that those who touched them should have had nothing in common, and those places . . .

Those places were *perfect.*

The worlds on the other side of their disparate doors were almost always perfect, fitting their young visitors like a bespoke glove fits the hand it was stitched for. "Almost always" is a very different thing from "always." Lives are lived and lost in "almost." Some of the children of the doors don't find perfection in the passage, and so are left exiles in a community of the exiled, unsure why they were chosen for a life-changing experience that failed to change them the same way it seemed to change everyone else it touched.

But even those whose doors had let them down would walk

with a hole in their heart for the rest of their days, not quite present and not quite gone, unable to fully rejoin the world they had begun in and then been banished back to. Misplacement was their commonality; exile was their community.

These were the things they all knew, the stories they shared. But for some, there was another lesson buried under the misplacement, an education in instances and errors. Those travelers learned not only what it meant to be mislaid, but what it meant to become so fundamentally and foundationally unanchored from who they had originally been that they could no longer find their way back to that person, even in the rare cases when they had the enviable luxury of a tether. For some, "mislaid" blossomed into "lost" before it swelled to become Lost, which sounded the same, yet was somehow utterly and completely different, a passport to a different country.

Mislaid things would, inevitably, turn up again, returned to their places, whether or not those places still fit them. Things that were merely lost could still be found, could be returned to where they belonged, because they truly belonged *somewhere.* A lost child might belong where they'd begun, or might belong in the world they'd traveled to, but either way, one of those places would hold and harbor them. One of those places could be home.

A Lost child could wander forever, destined only for the doors, could start and stop and start again a thousand times, and still they would be Lost, from the beginning to the end. Still they would be stumbling, still somehow stranded on that first threshold, in that instant between reaching out and reaching a destination.

The Lost understood the lost ones, for they had also begun among the mislaid. They had that in common. They still shared the similarities carried by all the children of the doors.

It was just that they didn't stop there, but continued onward, becoming something else. Something that was neither worse nor better, but was decidedly different.

Eleanor West had encountered a few of the Lost since opening her school, her Home for Wayward Children, and as they shared so much with their peers—as they had all been taken by the doors, voluntarily or no—if they were among the number she believed that she might be able to help find peace, she still welcomed them. She never once turned anyone away. Unlike the doors they had traveled through, the school's door was always open for the lost and the Lost alike, offering them a sanctuary for as long as they might need it. Her rules were simple, universal, and unambiguous:

No solicitation. No visitors.

No quests.

1 ARRIVALS

ELEANOR'S SCHOOL WAS ORGANIZED and patterned as only a school owned and at least technically operated by a true child of Nonsense could have been. The divisions between her students were less about age than they were experience, and as it was rare for two pupils to travel to the same world, even when the class rosters were studied over the span of several decades, those experiences were assessed more on conjecture than established fact. This perfectly suited Eleanor's Nonsensical way of thinking, which had been trained into topsy-turviness and encouraged to remain that way. So she put Nonsense with Nonsense, and Logic with Logic, and assigned those labels based on the stumbling accounts of traumatized children who had just been cast out of their own personal homelands, and called it good.

Was it any wonder that occasionally, she got the labels wrong?

Cora Miller was a temporarily land-bound mermaid who had fallen through a door that couldn't exist, a door suspended in hope and absence and shadows on the water, to find herself in a Drowned World deep beneath an endless sea. The closest label in Eleanor's book of worlds was a Lake, but Cora's Trenches had been so much bigger than any Lake. She had been swept out to sea, and if there was no classification for such a thing on the Compass, maybe it was because the children swept out to sea so very rarely survived the swim back to shore. Cora didn't talk much about the Trenches outside of therapy, but what she did say painted a land of endless tides, of predictable rhythms, of laws and rituals and deep, powerful customs.

So how was it that Eleanor, in all her experience and wisdom, had looked at the Trenches and marked them as a Nonsense world? And how was it that when Antoinette Ricci had appeared on the school steps of her own volition, with no parents to enroll her and no academic record to guide her placement, Eleanor had listened to her halting description of the Land Where the Lost Things Go and decided that it, too, must be Nonsense?

Antsy could almost see the logic there, if she squinted. The store where she'd traded her childhood for wild adventures had opened Doors onto countless worlds, each with their own laws both natural and artificial. It had been a nonsense place, solely because no form of order could have encompassed everything it was connected to. But if the nature of whatever was on the other side of a door could be said to flavor the character of the room a person stood in, there were no Logical worlds. There couldn't be. A single drop of Nonsense would be enough to pollute the whole system.

So Cora and Antsy, both of whom were Nonsense-but-not, both of whom had visited worlds with no cousin-cognates currently represented by the rest of the student body, were stuck rooming together, both trying to pretend it didn't bother them in the slightest, just trying to move from one day to the next without causing any problems.

They had been shoved together the day Antsy showed up at the school, a jangling, unsteady bundle of nerves, stomach heavy with the remains of the cheeseburger she'd bolted down at the bus stop, which had tasted amazing and somehow transformed into lead the second that it hit her stomach.

Not literal lead—this was Earth, after all, where all the magic was specks and spots clinging to children who'd passed through Doors of their own, only to return with parlor tricks in their hands and shadows in their hearts—but something close enough that by the time Eleanor had finished explaining the purpose of the school and the rules under which it operated, Antsy had been increasingly sure that she was going to be sick. She didn't *want* to be sick, had long since learned that the best meal was the one you didn't lose, but sometimes the realities of living in a body didn't match up well with what she wanted.

Still, she'd willingly gone with Eleanor to sit in her cozy, cluttered office and listen as Eleanor explained what would be expected of her if she was going to enroll in classes. Eleanor fascinated her. She looked old enough to be a grandmother, but she moved quickly, like someone much younger. Nothing about her made Antsy suspect her of trading time for adventure: Eleanor had lived every day she carried, and quite a few more beside.

"You're not the first who's come here with a name and an identity, but neither of them things that can be shared without legal difficulties," she'd said, voice kind and hands folded carefully on the desk. She spoke to Antsy like she was a wild thing that Eleanor wanted very badly not to frighten, keeping her tone low and never letting her pitch rise beyond a certain point. It was impressive, given the clear marks of Nonsense in her eyes and clothing. That, more than anything she was saying, told Antsy she had the experience she claimed. That she could *understand*.

"Now, to be quite clear, most of those travelers have come to us from worlds beyond this one, children of the doors whose paradise lay in more mundane directions than many of our own, but we've had others who were so changed by where they'd gone that they couldn't return to their old lives, even if they'd wanted to." The woman had paused then, tilting her head to the side like a magpie, and asked, "*Is* this the world where you were born?"

"Yes," Antsy had answered, and the tears, which she had managed to hold back for so impossibly long, had finally come, rising to her eyes and running down her cheeks in fat, heavy lines. "My name is Antoinette Ricci. My father's name was Joseph Ricci, and my mother's name is Mia, but I don't know her last name anymore. I have a little sister. Her name is Abigail, and I haven't seen her since she was still a baby, and I don't think I'm ever going to see her again. People call me Antsy."

"All right, Antsy," the woman had replied, and pushed a box of tissues across the desk toward Antsy. "You're allowed to cry here, as much as you need to. My name is Eleanor, and that's my name on the door, and this is my school. I own the house and the grounds and everything else around here, and you're not going to get into any trouble with anyone for being here. Now, you said your father's name *was* Joseph Ricci. Did something happen, sweetheart?"

"Yes," Antsy had said, and maybe that was the moment where she'd convinced Eleanor that she'd gone to a Nonsense world, because that one question marked the moment where she had begun to laugh. Her tears hadn't stopped, hadn't even really slowed, but oh, how the laughter had chased them out of her body, seeming to swallow her up completely.

Eleanor hadn't batted an eye, only watched in patient silence until both tears and laughter began to taper off. Then, and only then, she had sighed and said, "I won't ask until you choose to answer, but is anyone looking for you? Anyone at all?"

"No, ma'am. I don't think anyone is."

"That's a terrible thing for a child to carry, but in this circumstance, it may be for the best. Investigations are disruptive, and bad for the educational environment. Can you tell me how you found us? What brought you here?" She'd paused then, making a space for Antsy to speak. Antsy had never needed anyone to make spaces for her. When she hadn't been able to find them on her own, she had barged ahead and made them, whether or not people wanted her to. But in that moment, her head had gone empty, and her mouth had gone dry.

Everything she had to say was impossible. Everything she'd gone through was impossible. She was nine years old, with the body of someone on the high side of sixteen and the mind of . . . She didn't even know how old her thoughts were, and she didn't like to think about it. The idea that the Doors might have changed her mind while they were changing her body was too much to take, one more violation piled onto an endless tower that threatened to come crashing down and crush her flatter than anything. So when offered the opportunity to tell her story, she couldn't decide how she was supposed to begin.

Finally, the silence had become too heavy, and Eleanor had begun to speak again. "When I was a little girl, some of my cousins used to talk about how I'd had an aunt none of us ever had the opportunity to know," she'd said. "They didn't know her name, and they didn't know for sure whether she was an aunt or another cousin, one tied to the generation before ours, but her story was so delicious that they told it anyway. They said she had been willful and disobedient, that she had run away from her parents when she was meant to be doing the mending, run off to play in the woods like a wild thing. And some *other* wild thing had come and snatched her away, so completely that they never found her, and that was why none of us were allowed to go to the woods alone, no matter how responsible or careful we were.

"Well, I didn't care for hearing that one little bit, and so the next chance I was given, I snuck away to the woods—they were even nearer the house then than they are now, and they're near enough to the house now that some of the rooms can be reached from the trees, if you're the climbing kind. You look like you might be the climbing kind. Are you, Antsy?"

It was the sort of question that wasn't intended to receive an answer, and so Antsy hadn't given one, just kept looking at Eleanor in wide-eyed silence. Eleanor had smiled a little, like that was all the answer she could ever have asked for, and said, "I thought so. You'll be able to be happy here, if you allow it. So off I snuck to the woods, brave and bold as only a seven-year-old on an adventure can be. She was me and I was her, and sometimes I remember her so vividly I expect to see her waiting in my mirror. I suppose we all feel that way, when we've gotten old. Into the shadows of the trees I went, with their stained-glass leaves and their branches like reaching hands. I suppose I was trying to prove I was braver than my cousins, who thought they were better than me because they were older. I suppose I was trying to prove I wasn't afraid, even though anyone who saw me would have known that wasn't true. And I suppose I was trying to solve a mystery. Where did this cousin I'd never heard of before go? Why had we forgotten her as a family, when we could have been out looking for her in the wild places?

"I had so many questions that day, and what I found answered all of them and none of them and taught me that questions are like coats: you can turn them inside out when you need to hide from the fairies. Nothing sees you when you're cloaked in a question with its seams showing. I found a little space between the roots of a tree, the sort of space that only calls to children and other small creatures, and it looked like a doorway. It looked like it could be the passage into something wonderful and new, something I had never seen before. So I squirmed myself between the roots, and do you know what I found there?"

This was the sort of question that *did* ask for an answer, even though an answer should have been too impossible to occur to anyone. "Another door," Antsy had replied, slow and careful as anything. "Small, but big enough for you."

"Do you know what was *written* on the door?"

"*Be sure*. It asked you to be sure." Antsy had started to cry again then, even though it had been hard for her to notice after all the crying she'd already done, and she had looked at Eleanor, and wondered if this kind, smiling old woman had seen the Store, if she *understood*. "And then, one day, you weren't."

"Not quite, my darling, but close enough for corkscrews." Eleanor had stepped back around the desk and offered Antsy her hands. "Every door is a little different, and every world they take us to is *very* different indeed, but they all ask the same thing of us, and they all break our hearts, in the end."

"Did you ever find your cousin?" Antsy had asked, taking the offered hands and letting herself be tugged to her feet.

"Yes, and she didn't thank me for banishing her back to this world after so much time had passed, but that's neither here nor there, and as I didn't know what I was doing, I didn't do anything wrong. You don't have to tell anyone about your door if you don't want to, although you'll be asked to share in group, if you're comfortable. We're part school, part . . . readjustment center, let's call it, for people who've been to places like the ones we went to, and need a little help remembering what it's like to live in *this* world."

"I thought I *was* sure," Antsy had replied. "I thought I was so sure, of everything, and then I was back where I began."

But not really, not all the way: the Store had put her back where it had found her, restoring what had been taken into its keeping, but the things she'd lost while she was on the other side, those were gone forever. Those were payment due.

"If there's any doubt at all, the doors throw us back," Eleanor'd said. "But more than that, sometimes there are . . . other rules. Some doors are anchored. They allow for a certain amount of going back and forth on the part of the traveler. Other doors only appear for people who fit a list of requirements, and if even one thing changes, it's possible the door will decide you weren't who they wanted after all, thrust you out, and leave you. It's a terrible system. Cruel comfort, I know, but you won't be alone here. You *will* be expected to attend classes. It keeps the state from bothering us. Do you have any special skills?"

Antsy somehow knew that Eleanor wasn't asking about hopping on one foot for an especially long time or tying daisy stems into knots with her eyes closed. She'd opted for honesty. "I get . . . static . . . in my head sometimes. Like a radio that's not quite tuned to the channel it's supposed to be tuned to. When that happens, it's because there's something that wants to be found, and I can find anything. Anything at all."

"You would have been great help when I lost my keys," said Eleanor, in a flippant tone. "Come along, then. We'll get you sorted. Is there anything you *do* feel comfortable telling me about the world on the other side of your door?"

Antsy had stumbled her way through an explanation

of the Store, leaving out all the parts she knew a grownup wouldn't want to hear, and by the time they'd been halfway up the stairs to the second floor of the grand old home, Eleanor had declared gleefully that "Nonsense! It was all Nonsense, from one shelf to the next, and so you're a Nonsense girl, and I have just the perfect place for you."

2 GETTING SETTLED

THEN HAD COME THE top of the stairs, and then had come Cora, quiet, tragic Cora, who seemed to be slowly bleeding to death from a wound that no one, not even she, could see. Eleanor had informed Cora that Antsy was going to be her new roommate, and thus had the die been cast and the decision made.

For her part, Cora had accepted this intrusion with stolid good grace, as she seemed to accept almost everything, and while she didn't offer Antsy her hand in friendship, she wasn't cruel to her, either. As for Antsy, well, she didn't try to push the issue. She'd never been around girls her own age before. She didn't honestly know what that terrifying phrase, "her own age," was supposed to mean. So she watched Cora carefully, trying to figure out how to pass for what she appeared to be, trying to learn the tricks to moving among the teenage population of the school as one of their own.

They weren't the only students, of course: there were around twenty others. They ranged in age from thirteen to nineteen, divided into academic groups by tests and experience rather than age. Antsy was alone in what Eleanor called "the Basic Curriculum," trying to learn all the things she hadn't needed to know either as a nine-year-old girl or while she was effectively helping to run the Store, but which were now necessary here in the world where she'd been born.

"At least you can read and write and do your numbers,"

Eleanor had said, after the first time Antsy complained about being alone in the classroom. "We've had students who had been raised by wolves, or dreams, or dinosaurs, and didn't know much beyond how to say their own names. You'll catch up to the others in no time at all."

Antsy had been quiet after that, realizing that Eleanor thought she was worried about being forced to learn something below her grade level and not about being left alone. "I understand," she'd said, and that had been the end of that. Things moved on.

If Antsy had been required to summarize her first six months at the school, that's what she would have said: things moved on. She met her roommate, she abandoned attempts at friendship for the small luxury of friendliness, and things moved on. She met the other students, including Cora's *actual* friends: Kade, with his steady, calming personality, the oldest student currently at the school, who never willingly spoke of the world on the other side of his door; Sumi, who was exactly the opposite of either steady or calming, whose parents were dead and who talked about the time she'd been murdered and resurrected in the same airy, careless tone she used when explaining why maple syrup was a natural topping for spaghetti and meatballs, why wouldn't you want a little sweet with your savory?; Christopher, who was quick and cool and careful, who carried a flute made of bone that only Sumi could hear him play. They were far from the only students, but they were the ones who worried about Cora, who came to the room to try and lure her out, who made note of Antsy if only as a change to the landscape, and whose easy acceptance of her presence made settling in at the school less difficult than it could have been.

Leaving Cora's narrow circle of friends, Antsy went looking for Angela, the girl whose kitten had been lost. Finding it had given Antsy the first clue she needed to reach the school. "I met your mother," she'd said, haltingly, on the day in the cafeteria when she approached the brown-haired girl with the companion so heart-stoppingly beautiful that Antsy couldn't look at her directly.

Not that Antsy wanted to. From the way her eyes refused to focus on the girl who walked with Angela, she was fairly sure she knew the world she'd been to visit. It had never been kind to visitors, and the one time Antsy had opened a Door there, even Vineta had been unwilling to let her pass through to the other side.

Angela had blinked, very slowly and deliberately, as if Antsy's proclamation were the rudest thing imaginable, and then she'd asked, "Why do I care?" while her companion tittered, and Antsy had walked away from them knowing she'd find no friendship there. Then again, she hadn't been expecting it. The static would have led her to them, if they'd been what she was here to find.

Six months of long, boring classes, slightly more engaging therapy sessions that felt almost more like fairy-tale story circles, and waking in the middle of the night to Cora's screams. The blue-haired girl's invisible wound was bleeding faster and faster, and Antsy didn't see any way that she could help her. Antsy was still getting used to shoes and schedules and dental floss and all the other little ephemera of being back in the "real" world.

Roughly a month after she showed up at the school, Kade had produced a small plastic rectangle with her picture and a bunch of lies on it. On the name line, it said "Antoinette West." Antsy had looked at him curiously, the rectangle in her hand, and he had shrugged, suddenly awkward.

"Auntie said you couldn't use your last name because

people might be looking for you, but that you're not one of the ones we have to keep hidden and pretend isn't here," he'd said. "She seemed to think no one would be able to recognize you if they saw you. That so?"

Antsy had nodded, wondering how much she'd accidentally let slip. Did Eleanor somehow know how old she actually was? Or did she think that Antsy was like Cora, and her hair had changed color on the other side of the door? But those hadn't been questions she could ask, and so she had simply nodded, tucking the rectangle into her pocket where it would be safe.

"Don't lose that," Kade had said. "We've got a former student who makes IDs for us when we need him to, but he costs, and he doesn't like to have too many floating around out there. It took a while to get this one arranged."

Antsy scoffed. "I don't lose anything," she'd said.

"That's what Auntie says. Welcome to the family, cuz," and he'd grinned, all sharp white teeth and amusement, and Antsy had grinned back, feeling suddenly free. Little rectangles with everything there was to know about a person were a sort of currency in this world. They meant you existed all the way, so even the computers knew you were there. And if she had the same last name as Eleanor and Kade, that meant she had a family again. Last names could change, and being a part of a family didn't mean people wouldn't hurt you, but it was still something wonderful.

But the little rectangle had stayed in her pocket, never used, until the day she'd woken up to find Cora already gone, and not soaking in the bathtub as she often did on the quiet mornings, when the bones of the school rattled in the fading wind, when the ghosts in the walls—not literal ghosts, not that Antsy had ever been able to tell, but ghosts all the same, ghosts made of absence, of loneliness and longing—came out and wept. The static had been there to fill the space where Cora wasn't, and so Antsy had gone creeping around the school, letting the lodestone ache of something needing to be found lead her, until she'd left the school entirely to go walking across the dew-wet yard into the trees, which were as close and dense and yes, old, as Eleanor had said they were.

Into the woods she'd gone, one whisper-quiet slip of a teenage girl with red, red hair and a long pink nightgown getting muddy at the hem, following a static only she could hear. She'd been passing a particularly tall and gnarled tree when the static changed, going from a low buzz to a ringing in her ears so loud that it almost hurt. Recognizing a prod when she felt one, she had turned toward the tree, kneeling in its roots.

There, tucked between two thick old roots each as big around as her arm, was a tunnel. If she squinted, she could just barely see a Door at the very end of it, small and golden-brown and almost glowing, although it didn't cast any noticeable light. It was simply more visible than it should have been, given everything around it.

"No, thank you," she had said, something close to terror building in her chest. For six months she'd gone to bed and woken up only a night's sleep older. For six months she'd lived minute to minute, day to day, aging at exactly the same speed as everyone around her. She could tell, just by looking, that this Door wasn't the one that would take her back to the Store. This Door belonged to Eleanor.

More, she could tell that it had somehow lingered, that it had been exactly where it was now for a very long time. Long enough for the tree to grow around it, rather than wedging itself into an open spot in the world. This Door had been before the school; it very well might be after, as well.

Antsy remembered the things they'd been told in evening therapy sessions, about how most Doors appeared once, then vanished forever, or as good as forever, and how some of them stayed until they were opened, and how some—the rarest of them all—put down roots and stayed close enough to forever as to mean the very same thing. She thought about some of the things she'd heard murmured about Eleanor, about the hungry way their headmistress watched Sumi move through the school, about the way she tried to assign every new student to Nonsense, whether or not it suited their narrative, and thought she understood something now that she hadn't before waking up alone in her room.

The ringing faded, replaced by the static that had drawn her out here to begin with, and she scrabbled around in the dirt until her fingers hit something hard and sharp and neither stick nor stone. Antsy pulled whatever it was out of the dirt, holding it up to see in the watery moonlight. A ring of keys, complete with ancient, moldy rabbit's foot.

And then it was off to the office with something new known and something to return. Doors had their own song in the static; if she was close to finding one of them, they screamed to be seen. But other things would still sing when it was time to bring them home.

Antsy had returned the keys to Eleanor just in time to catch the fact that Cora had requested a relocation, and she'd gone back to their still-shared room sick with the conviction that she must have done something wrong at some point during their brief time together. She'd slipped somehow, said something she shouldn't have, and now even her roommate couldn't stand to be around her.

Intellectually, she knew she'd done nothing of the sort, but emotionally, she was struggling to behave like as old as she looked. She had no idea how most things worked, and she was getting overwhelmed easily and often, bending under the weight of a world she no longer understood. If there was blame in the offing, even imagined blame, it was easier to take it on her own shoulders.

Three days later, Cora was gone, bound for the foreboding-sounding Whitethorn Institute with its promise to "cure" students of the "delusions" which had severed them from their lives and families.

Two days after *that*, Cora's friends had come to Antsy, saying they'd heard she could find anything. They wanted her to find their friend.

She had agreed, and Cora had come home, along with Sumi and a small cluster of new faces, Regan and Julia and Carrie and Emily and Marian, and Antsy suspected—although she couldn't quite be sure—that was when everything had started to go wrong.

3 HIDE AND SEEK IS LOST AND FOUND FOR AMATEURS

"I HEARD YOU CAN find anything," said Emily anxiously, standing near where Antsy sat in the school cafeteria, a former dining room that had been converted to hold forty students eating at once. All the escapees from Whitethorn were like that: anxious. They sounded worried all the time, like they knew down to the bottom of their bones that any day now, they'd be gathered up and carried back to what Antsy thought sounded very much like a prison.

They also didn't know how to be free anymore. They flirted with the idea like guests at a party, taking little steps and stabs, then dancing backward, out of reach. The more regimented things could be, the more relaxed they were. Eleanor had assigned one of them, Julia, to teach Antsy's classes, and the woman could barely answer questions that weren't precisely outlined in the text.

"Barely" wasn't the same as "couldn't," though, and Antsy could see flickers of rebellion in Julia's expression during class. It was Julia, always Julia, no "Miss" or "ma'am" attached. The one time Antsy had called her "Miss Julia," the woman had recoiled so violently that she smacked her head against the wall, and classes had been cancelled for the rest of the day.

A new teacher wasn't the only change brought on by Cora's return. Cora hadn't come back to room with Antsy, instead moving into Sumi's room, although all three of them quietly agreed that the Trenches hadn't been Nonsense at all.

That world of watery wonders was Logic by any reasonable definition, and it was odd that Eleanor had been able to get that wrong. Although she'd been wrong about the Store, too.

So for the time being, Antsy slept and woke alone, waiting for the day when the slow shuffle of rooms would put someone new into the bed across from hers, which was slowly becoming a dumping ground for clean but unfolded laundry, vanishing under shirts and sweaters.

"I can," Antsy agreed, with her own note of wariness. "You have your lunch?"

Emily nodded.

"Sit down, then." And she'd scooted her own tray closer to herself, making space as Emily sat.

Lunch and breakfast at the school were informal affairs, as much buffet as menu, with the students free to pick and choose from whatever suited them. Antsy looked at the contents of Emily's tray, blinking a bit at the jumble. Wholegrain bread smeared with butter and what looked like cranberry relish, a slice of pumpkin pie, and half an acorn squash dusted with cinnamon and sugar.

Emily saw her looking and blushed, already dark cheeks growing darker. "I know it's a little weird, but it's what I like, and Sumi said I was allowed to have whatever I liked for lunch. I'll eat the same as everyone else does at dinner, I promise."

"Oh, I don't care what you eat," said Antsy. "It just reminded me of this holiday we used to celebrate when I was little, with the whole family and a roast turkey and stuffing my grandmother would make from bread she'd baked the day before. I don't remember what it was called, though. Do you remember that holiday?"

Emily looked at her with careful suspicion. "Are you making fun of me?" she asked. "I'm American too, you know. I was born in Minneapolis."

Antsy blinked. "Is there a reason I would be making fun of you?"

"Maybe. You never can tell who's going to turn out to be the sort of person who tells you to go back where you came from, like all the white people didn't come here from someplace else to begin with." Emily's shoulders untensed, and she reached, still cautious, for her fork. "Yeah, we had Thanksgiving."

"Thanksgiving! That was the name!" Antsy snapped her fingers, grinning—a grin which faded as she realized, only a second later, that the word was gone again. "Oh, darn. I hoped it would stick."

Emily was staring at her. "Hoped what would stick?"

"I was in a market square in . . . a place very, very far away from here, and when an old merchant said she could teach me the word that unlocked every door, I said I wanted it," said Antsy matter-of-factly. "She said she wanted the names of all the holidays I'd ever celebrated with my family, and we didn't have holidays where I was, so it didn't feel particularly important. Still doesn't, most of the time."

Emily's stare slowly morphed into a look of horror. "So you don't remember *any* of the holidays you had with your family?"

"Nope." Antsy shrugged. "It doesn't bother me much. I still remember the *holidays,* and what they felt like. They just don't have names to keep them in focus. There was the one with all the food, and the one with the presents and the home invasion, and the one with the giant rabbit."

"You forgot Halloween," said Emily.

Antsy looked at her blankly. "I'm sorry. That name doesn't mean anything to me."

"Halloween," said Emily again, more firmly. "It's the best holiday of the whole year. It's costumes and candy and everyone's all the way the same, because no one knows who you are. There's no rich kids or poor kids on Halloween, no one being a jerk just because they don't like that you're better than them in dance class when they think your skin's not the right color for a prima ballerina—like skin has anything to do with dancing, like being white makes up for having no discipline when it comes to practice—it's just skeletons and hayrides and this taste in the back of your throat like candy corn and bonfire smoke and apple cider all mixed together."

"Oh," said Antsy, and then, more firmly, "*Oh.* I remember that night. My daddy took me trick-or-treating, said we could watch scary movies together when I was older, but not until I was old enough to help him keep Mommy from being frightened. There was candy, and I wore an orange dress and a black hat with glitter on it, and told everyone who asked what a wicked witch I was. I even cackled, like this—" And she laughed, a high and cackling laugh that would have been right at home behind a bubbling cauldron.

Emily didn't look concerned. If anything, her expression softened, some of the horror leaching away and replaced by something that looked almost like contentment. "Just like that," she said. "Everyone's a monster on Halloween, and that means no one's a monster, and if there aren't any monsters, you get to decide what 'monster' means."

"There's a word," said Sumi, plopping down next to Emily with her own tray. Her lunch was a riot of brightly colored candy and three kinds of cake, which might not have looked quite so appalling if she hadn't tied the whole mess together with a lazy spiral of whipped cream and rainbow sprinkles. "Or I guess it's a phrase, really. 'Semantic satiation.' It means when you say the same thing too many times it stops meaning anything. I think you just said 'monster' so many times that now it means the same thing as 'mashed potato.' Treat or trick!"

Emily frowned at her. "It's 'trick or treat,' Sumi."

"Okay!" Sumi dipped a hand into her pocket and produced a blue-wrapped KitKat with pink flowers printed on the outside, dropping it onto Emily's tray. She narrowly missed the acorn squash. "You working your way around to asking for your big favor?"

"Shush," said Emily.

"Haven't yet," said Sumi. She turned a broad, somewhat unnerving smile on Antsy.

Sumi was a lot smarter than she tried to seem, and Antsy knew better than to believe she was here by coincidence, any more than Emily was. The Whitethorn escapees had a tendency to stick together, and Emily had never come up to her at lunch before, much less tried to have a real conversation. She picked up her sandwich—tuna on white bread, one of the most decadent things she could think of—and nibbled at a corner, waiting for one or both of them to get on with it.

Emily squirmed, appearing to realize that if she didn't get to whatever point she was dancing around, Sumi would get there for her. She shifted to face Antsy straight on, sitting up straight and leveling her shoulders until her posture was unquestionably perfect. "I heard you can find anything," she repeated.

"That's exactly what you said instead of 'hello,'" said

Antsy, not putting down her sandwich. "Word for word. Do you have a *script*?"

"I was wondering—I mean, some of us were wondering—do you charge? Could I pay you to find something for me?"

"I haven't charged so far; it would seem wrong, I guess, unless you were asking me to find something for a mean reason, or that I'm not supposed to look for. If you asked me to find Sumi's diary, I would probably charge you for *that*. Also, I wouldn't do it."

"Unless your 'finding anything' reaches all the way to finding things that don't exist, you're not going to find my diary," said Sumi, fishing a cupcake out of the mess on her tray. It dripped whipped cream on the table as she added, "Or my underwear," in a suggestive tone.

"I do not want to know about your underwear," said Antsy.

"Your loss," said Sumi, and rose, wandering away. She left her rainbow nightmare of a lunch behind.

"I'm sorry about her," said Emily, clearly trying to salvage whatever she'd been trying to accomplish. "She's been in a mood all morning, since Kade said he wanted to go over the admissions from the last year with Carrie and Julia. He thinks too many students have been getting filed as Nonsense, and it's skewing his map of the Compass."

"And Sumi doesn't like the idea of the Nonsense kids losing their numerical advantage," said Antsy. "Makes sense." Hopefully, this would get the Store moved to someplace on the map that made more sense. Then she could start thinking about the Compass like it actually reflected reality, even if it was only a little bit.

"Which is another thing Sumi doesn't like," said Emily. She picked up the KitKat, frowning at the wrapper. "'Sakura-flavored'? It tastes like cherry trees?"

"How is that any stranger than maple syrup?"

"Oh, you did *not* just call maple syrup strange," said Emily. "Maple syrup is the blood of the divine, boiled down into perfection, and you will not impugn it in my presence!"

Antsy laughed, and there were no more scripts as both of them finished their lunch, chatting about holidays she didn't remember and scary movies she hadn't seen, and when the bell rang for the next period, she felt as if she'd both made a friend and played a successful prank—a trick to go with the treat of their conversation. Emily hadn't seemed to realize how different they were, age-wise, and maybe that meant no one ever would. Maybe she could get away with what she couldn't change.

It wasn't until she was settling alone at her desk in the classroom where the Basic Curriculum was taught to her class of one that she realized Emily had never told her what she wanted Antsy to find.

4 A DANGEROUS TALENT

EVENINGS WERE MOSTLY taken up by therapy sessions, frequently uncomfortable events where groups of students in different combinations were ushered into a room to share their experiences. The woman who ran them, Nichole, was pleasant, about the age of Antsy's mother, and seemingly unflappable. She was door-touched like the rest of them—most members of the staff were, one way or another, although some were kin to travelers, rather than former travelers in their own right, and a few of the teachers who covered only one class or subject had no idea that this was anything other than a very strange boarding school.

"The locals think we're sort of like juvie light," Sumi had said once, tossing a ball of yarn up into the air again and again, catching it like a cat. "They figure we're all messed up, and that this is a good, controlled place for us to reintegrate into society."

"Doesn't that bother you?" Antsy had replied. She didn't like the idea of people thinking she was "messed up," whatever that meant.

"No, 'cause they're right" had been Sumi's reply. "None of us is normal, and we'll either figure out how to pretend we are, or we'll find our doors home, and then we won't have to worry about it anymore, because all the ways we're not normal are the way our real homes want us to be. We're perfectly normal in the right environment."

She had wandered away then, and that conversation replayed in Antsy's mind every time she approached the room where group was held. Tonight was for students whose worlds had touched on what Eleanor called the "minor" directions, aspects of their realities that were harder to classify than the broad questions of Nonsense, Logic, Virtue, and Wickedness.

While Eleanor had been quick to declare the Store a Nonsense world, Antsy had spoken with Kade while he was helping her get a wardrobe together, and he had decided it needed to be added to columns labeled "Linearity" and "Whimsy."

Shoulders tight, Antsy slipped into the room and looked for an open chair around the outside of the circle. Only about half the seats were occupied; the Nonsense and Logic nights tended to be chaotic and sometimes uncomfortably loud, but the minor directions never attracted many people.

Group was optional for anyone who'd been at the school for a year or more. Antsy was thus used to not seeing many of the people she considered friends even on the major nights, and the minors were usually just her with a therapist and a bunch of kids she barely knew.

Even if you did attend, no one was required to share. Antsy knew even before she sat down that this wasn't going to be one of the nights when she joined the conversation. She had slept poorly the night before; the branches rattling outside her window had woken her several times, surfacing, gasping, in her silent room. The silence made her miss Cora more. They weren't *friends,* not the way she was friends with Sumi or Christopher, whose dry sense of humor delighted her, but they'd been companionable in their silences, and she liked having someone around.

She was so preoccupied with thinking about how much she hoped for a new roommate that she didn't notice someone sitting in the chair to her left.

"Psst," said a voice.

A girl whose name Antsy didn't know was at the front of the room next to Nichole, head bowed and hands clasped, talking about a world of moths and moonlight, where everything happened according to the verses of something she called the "Great Song." Apparently, she had been asked to write new text, and had been gathering the ingredients for ink when she stumbled back into her own backyard. She was afraid of what would happen if she didn't get back before the written text ran out. Antsy blinked, shaking off the cobwebs of contemplation, and focused on the girl's story. She hadn't realized she'd been distracted enough to miss the start of the session.

"Psst," said the voice again.

Antsy leaned forward, twisting to see who was being so disrespectful. Letting her mind wander was rude but not actively disruptive. This, though. This was taking someone else's time and spending it as if it were your own, and that was a step beyond anything reasonable.

Angela raised one hand in a little wave, closing her fingers one after the other and opening them again the same way. Then she gestured toward the door. "Come on," she mouthed.

Antsy shook her head no.

Angela frowned, clearly having expected an easy acquiescence from the newer girl. She leaned farther forward. "Seraphina is waiting for us," she whispered.

Antsy shook her head again, this time wrinkling her nose in her best attempt at a "Who cares?" expression.

"You can't be serious," whispered Angela, somewhat more loudly. "She doesn't wait for *anyone*. She barely waits for *me*."

Antsy, who was more interested in following rules than in getting in good with the popular kids, shrugged.

"Get *up*," hissed Angela, barely whispering at all.

"Is there something wrong?" asked Nichole, her normally sweet and pleasant voice cracking through the room like the hand of all adult authority. The girl from the moth world was crying, hands covering half her face. Antsy cringed.

Angela, catching Antsy's reaction, smirked just a little. "Antoinette doesn't feel good, ma'am," she said. "She ate some potato salad with her dinner that I *told* her looked sort of nasty, but she didn't listen. I was trying to get her to let me take her to her room."

Nichole looked to Ansty, who was shrinking back in her seat, looking so unrelentingly miserable that it was easy to believe the lie of her illness. "Do you feel like you're going to be sick?" Nichole asked. She glanced back to the student who'd been speaking, then shifted her attention to Antsy. "Or do you feel like you need to see the doctor?"

The school didn't currently have a medical professional on staff, but all the adult teachers were trained in CPR and basic first aid. Nichole could hand out ibuprofen and antacids, and knew how to assess common ailments and decide whether something needed a trip to the local hospital or urgent care.

Agreeing would have been enough to get Antsy away from Angela. But it would also have meant telling the whole room she was sick when she *wasn't,* and being sick could mean doing really awful, embarrassing things, like throwing up or peeing in her pants. If she'd actually been sixteen, actually been sick, she might have been able to do it anyway.

Or, more likely, she might have been able to tell the adult that Angela was lying, and she wasn't sick at all, without the fear of upsetting someone she still saw as an older girl. So she bit her lip and shook her head, dismissing the offer as quickly as it had been made.

"Well, if you want to go lie down, I'll come check on you in a little bit," said Nichole.

Before Antsy could speak, Angela took Antsy's arm and stood. She was the taller of the two by an easy four inches, and had a runner's build, all long muscle and trained potential; she easily pulled Antsy to her feet.

"Sorry to have disrupted everyone," she said. "Sorry, Talia. Sorry, everybody. Come on, Antoinette."

She hauled Antsy along with her as she made for the door, and in seconds, they were in the hall. Angela didn't let go or slow down, but kept pulling Antsy until they reached the library, a massive, rectangular room whose walls were lined in shelves, each packed to capacity with an eclectic assortment of books. The floor was a maze of tables and chairs, all shoved around by students to fit whatever seating plan came into their heads; they were never returned to their original positions.

Antsy had never seen an adult in the library. Supposedly, the school had a librarian on staff, but Antsy had never seen one, only Mrs. Fetterman, who taught English and did all the ordering.

Seraphina was waiting there.

She was sitting in a high-backed, overstuffed armchair with her back to the fireplace, which painted the edges of her in a warm golden glow and left the rest of her in merciful shadow. Antsy thought she could almost make out the outlines of Seraphina's face, almost see the other girl for who she was, and not for the radiant haze of beauty that surrounded her wherever she walked. Only almost, though. Like the picture she'd seen on Angela's mother's refrigerator, Seraphina's edges remained blurred, refusing to be clearly seen.

"What *took* you so long?" demanded Seraphina, and there was nothing beautiful about her angry, waspish voice, which was tight and pinched off, making an accusation into an attack. It could have *been* beautiful—Antsy thought every voice could be beautiful, if it was used the right way—but it had no interest in beauty. It was like Seraphina, denied any other way to be unattractive, had channeled it all into her voice.

"I'm sorry," said Angela, letting Antsy go. Antsy remained where she was, frozen in the middle of the library, unable to muster the nerve to turn and run away. "She didn't want to come with me for some reason."

"Do you have any idea how hard it was to find a night when she wouldn't have one of her little inner circle of selfish *questers* keeping an eye on her?" Seraphina leaned forward, until the firelight was shining on her face, and her voice wasn't ugly at all. It was as beautiful as a mountain in the morning, perfectly shaped and sculpted and exactly the way it was supposed to be. No one with any sense would think anything about someone so totally perfect could be ugly.

Very distantly, Antsy was aware that this was Seraphina's "parlor trick." She was so beautiful that she could get anything she wanted, as long as she would just keep looking at you, keep paying attention to you, keep making you feel like the most important person in the world just because she thought you mattered enough to notice.

Angela was watching their interaction with something like awe and something like longing, blended together into a complicated emotion Antsy didn't recognize. She wasn't sure she'd recognize her own face in a mirror if she saw it just now. Whatever face she saw would be unutterably hideous, because she would still be seeing Seraphina's image dancing behind her eyes, chasing every other bit of beauty out of the world.

"She's here now, Sera," said Angela, a fawning note in her voice.

"Yes, she is," said Seraphina, keeping her eyes on Antsy.

It's like a snake charmer, thought Antsy. *If she stops giving me all her attention, she'll lose me, and I don't think she can get me again, not the same way she got me this time.*

That didn't change things, any more than knowing the world Seraphina had gone to did. A weapon's a weapon, whether or not you know its name. Antsy remained frozen as Seraphina rose and walked toward her, every step a celebration of movement, every gesture so unutterably perfect that it hurt.

"Hello, Antoinette," she purred, and for a moment, Antsy felt like she might actually die. "My name's Seraphina. I don't think we've met properly, have we? I'm sure I would have remembered a girl as pretty as you."

"It's the hair, it's just the hair, I'd be plain as paper without it, you're beautiful," stammered Antsy.

Seraphina laughed. "I am, aren't I? But what I'm not, in this world, is *real*. I'm so beautiful that no one can focus long enough to teach me anything, and no one can treat me impartially. All the teachers give me perfect grades, even when I turn in blank pieces of paper. The only person in this world who's ever told me no left a long time ago, thanks to the only person who's ever raised a hand against me. At least on the other side of my door, I had a chance. I could have a *life*. A person can't live like this. You can't be a person when you never have to work for anything, can you?"

"N-no," said Antsy. That seemed to be the answer Seraphina

wanted, and when she was rewarded with a smile, it felt like her heart was going to burst.

"No," said Seraphina. "You can't. You can't fall in love, because whoever you love will love you just because you want them to, and not because they want to. You can't have a job, because who would ever ask you to *work*? And you can't be *real*. But you're going to help me."

"H-how?" asked Antsy.

"You can find anything," said Seraphina, and for a moment, the echo of Emily in the cafeteria almost broke through Antsy's enthrallment, almost allowed her to step away.

Only almost. "I can," she dreamily agreed.

"Anything at all."

"If it exists, I can find it," said Antsy. "I can find lost socks and lost kittens and all sorts of things. But they have to really be real. I can't find time after you lose track of it. That would be silly."

"And no one here is ever silly, is that right?" asked Seraphina, and laughed when Antsy nodded enthusiastically. "See, Angela? It was always this easy. All we had to do was get her away from her little crew of self-appointed minders."

"I don't think she realized they were watching her," said Angela. "I think she thought they were her *friends*."

Seraphina laughed again, and there was a note of cruelty there that all the beauty in the world couldn't counteract.

"Why in the world would she have friends?" she asked. "Antisocial little loner in her very own remedial courses. She doesn't need *friends*. She needs a minder who can tell her who her real friends are. She needs us."

"She sure does," said Angela.

"Now, Antsy, I told you that you were going to help me,"

said Seraphina. "And you are. You're going to help me more than anyone else has, ever."

"How?" asked Antsy.

"You're going to find my door."

5 INTO THE STRANGE, DARK PLACES

ANTSY BOTH DID AND didn't want to do what Seraphina asked. She wanted to make Seraphina happy. But she was pretty sure that even if she *found* Seraphina's door, the other girl would demand Antsy be the one to open it, rather than trusting her. Almost as much as Antsy wanted to help Seraphina, she wanted to stay someone who got older at the same speed as everyone around her, not someone who was chasing adulthood like a dog chasing a rabbit. Most of all, she wanted to never open another Door. Some days she missed it so much it ached, like all her hands had ever been intended to do was reach for doorknobs, all her arms were for was to pull them open, and her legs, oh, those only existed to carry her through.

Those two warring wants crashed together in the middle of her heart, sending up a wall.

"She's fighting me," said Seraphina. "Isn't that adorable? She's fighting like she thinks she can *win*."

The wall was coming down. It had only been a clash of contradictions, and it couldn't last for long.

The final bit was crumbling away when the lights in the library went out, leaving them bathed in only firelight, and Antsy stumbled backward, gasping like she'd been struck. She could still *see* Seraphina, but with the fire to her back, the girl wasn't as inescapably beautiful as she'd been in full light. She was still pretty enough to be unnaturally compelling.

She wasn't pretty enough to force someone to do something they truly didn't want to do.

"Angela, what the *hell*?" demanded Seraphina.

"I didn't do it!" said Angela.

Someone grabbed Antsy's hand. She squeaked in surprise.

"Be quiet, new girl," snapped Seraphina.

Antsy didn't say anything as the person holding her hand tugged her away from the squabbling girls, or when Christopher's voice hissed, "Come on," next to her ear. Instead, she relaxed and nodded, trusting him to get her away.

Either Christopher could see in the dark or he had memorized the ever-shifting layout of the library, because he steered her around chairs, tables, and low shelves without hesitation, leading her to a door that had been half-hidden behind one of the larger shelves. "Through here," he murmured, "But it's going to let the light in. They may see us. Is your head clear enough to let you run?"

"I *think* so," said Antsy.

"Good. Make like Eurydice, and don't look back."

Antsy could hear the two girls pursuing them through the library, bumping into chairs and tables, Seraphina swearing every time she stubbed a toe or barked a shin. "I won't," she said fervently.

The dim shape that was Christopher nodded. Then he was pushing a door open, letting real light flood into the room. Antsy's eyes had barely had time to adjust to the shadows in the library, but they still burned for a moment as they remembered what it was to see. Christopher's hand was on her back, urging her forward, and she went willingly, stumbling into that well-lit space.

Cora was there. Solid, melancholic Cora, who looked her

up and down with quick efficiency. "Did they hurt you?" she asked.

Antsy shook her head.

Cora exhaled. "Good. I didn't think they would take their little mean-girl routine that far, but it's hard to tell where someone will stop when they think they're about to get the thing they want most in the world. Come on."

"Aren't we going to wait for Christopher?" asked Antsy.

"He's a big boy, he can get away from the terrible twosome if they give him a problem, and he knows where we're going. Come on." Unlike Angela and Christopher, Cora beckoned for Antsy to follow rather than grabbing her hand, and Antsy found herself oddly grateful for that, even as she followed Cora down the hall and up a narrow flight of stairs she'd never seen before.

"This place is no Winchester Mystery House, but Eleanor's parents were big rich, and so were their parents; this was the sort of ridiculous monument to generational wealth that you find in some of the old oil and lumber families," said Cora, as they climbed. "They built the original house, and as the family grew, they kept building. Then, after it was down to just Eleanor and some cousins, she turned it into a school, and *she* kept building, too, until she reached what she thought was the maximum size she could handle by herself. Not that she does most of the day-to-day handling. She has a whole team of lawyers and property managers who make sure the taxes get paid and the grounds are kept up. But since the building is so old, we have a bunch of stairways and doors that were meant for the help, and Eleanor never thinks to include them on the orientation map."

"Maybe she just thinks it's fun to have a bunch of hidden passages for the students to find," Antsy suggested.

"Maybe." Cora glanced back at her. "Why didn't you find them?"

"Oh. I can find things when I *need* them, personally—like I found Angela's kitten, which meant I found her mother, which meant I found out the school existed, and I needed to be here so I could be safe. And I can find things when people mention wanting me to look for them, or when I decide to look for them. But just being around something that's lost or hidden doesn't mean I'll automatically find it. Not unless I somehow know I ought to be looking."

"How the hell did she think you were Nonsense, even for a minute?" Cora sounded frustrated. "That's a lot of rules, and they'd have to be consistent for you to rattle them off that easily."

"I didn't tell her everything," said Antsy uncomfortably. "I didn't feel . . . It wasn't right, you know? Not yet. She wouldn't have understood. And so maybe what I *did* say made it easy for her to think that the Store was Nonsense. I don't know."

"Don't blame yourself," said Cora, pausing as she reached the top of the stairs. "She's seeing what she wants to see. She's been doing that more and more lately. Through here."

The stairs had ended at a door. Cora opened it, and Antsy followed her into the third-floor hallway. The students who'd been at the school longest were housed here, all except Sumi, who was on the second floor for the sake of the trees, and Christopher, who was in the basement for the sake of the shadows. Antsy didn't come this high very often. She'd never needed to.

Somewhat more concerningly, Seraphina's room was on this floor. Cora gave her a reassuring look.

"Christopher's still dealing with them, or he'd have met us here. We're almost to the attic."

"We're going to see Kade?"

"Kade was the one who asked the rest of us to keep an eye on you—well, Kade, and Sumi, who says she can see a quest taking root before it knows it's been planted. I'm not sure she's kidding about that. Seems like every time something weird happens, she's right at the middle of it." Cora snorted laughter. "Like anything at this school could be called 'weird' in comparison to anything else."

The attic door was small compared to the doors around it, which led into proper rooms and had thus been allotted more space in the hallway. An almost-polite sign reading KEEP OUT hung at eye level, which had always struck Antsy as odd, since Kade wasn't that antisocial. He managed the school wardrobe, collecting and cataloging any castoffs, as well as hand-making special items for people who could pay. He took money, favors—usually chores around the school— and information, as he tried to chart as accurate a map of the worlds as he could.

He would understand that a Nexus was neither Nonsense or Logic but something entirely its own, straddling the lines in a way too nuanced for most worlds to manage. It was fascinating how hard people from Earth seemed to find that idea, since Earth was a Nexus too, but Antsy supposed it was hard to look at your own nose. Still, if anyone would be able to hear her talk about the Store and really *listen,* it was probably Kade.

She should have come to him months ago, and realizing that as she waited for Cora to knock made her feel foolish. She shrank back as Cora lifted her hand, suddenly gripped by the urge to turn and run, and was on the verge of doing it when the static lit up at the back of her mind and she froze, trying to figure out what she was supposed to be looking for.

Cora knocked. The door opened. Kade must have been waiting for them. The static got stronger. He smiled as he saw Antsy.

"Hey, Antsy. You all right?"

Antsy nodded. "Angela told a lie to get me out of group, and then she took me to where Seraphina was waiting, in the library, and Seraphina got real close to me so I couldn't not see how pretty she was, and told me I was going to find her door. I didn't want to, so I pushed back as hard as I could, but she was *so* pretty, and I was about to say I'd do it when the lights went out."

"Christopher," said Cora.

Kade turned his smile to her. "Makes sense. Boy does like a simple solution. Come on, Antsy. We've been waiting for you to be comfortable enough to join us, and since we've run out of time to wait, we need to go."

He turned then, heading up the narrow flight of stairs to the attic, and Cora gestured for Antsy to follow.

Kade stepped to the side at the top of the stairs to let Antsy pass, and she emerged into the wonderland that was his room. He'd been at the school so long that his environment had been completely reshaped to suit him, books and bolts of cloth piled in semblance of furniture. The only piece of real furniture in sight was the table where he kept his sewing machine; Antsy wasn't sure he even had a *bed*.

Sumi was sitting on one of the piles of books, if anyone could call lying on her back with her legs in the air, ankles crossed and feet propped against a wardrobe, *sitting*. She had a length of ribbon in her hands, and was weaving it through

her fingers in an intricate design that Antsy recognized but couldn't quite place. Emily was on the floor next to her, Sumi's inverted pigtails just barely brushing her shoulders, her legs stretched out in front of her and her toes pointed at the far wall. She looked up sharply at the sound of footsteps, and looked faintly embarrassed when Antsy appeared.

"I'm so sorry," Emily said. "This is all my fault."

"Fault's like salt, it spreads around," said Sumi dismissively.

"She's right," said Kade, as he followed Antsy into the attic and moved aside again, this time so Cora could come up. "Emily, you didn't do anything wrong, you just asked a question we were still trying to put together. And you wouldn't even have known to do that if you hadn't heard us talking about it."

"And you wouldn't have heard us talking about it if I hadn't gone and enrolled in Whitethorn to get Cora back where she belongs, and hauled you out for good measure," said Sumi.

Emily flinched. "Don't *ever* talk like you shouldn't have done that," she said, hotly. "Don't *ever*. I was dying in there."

"And now you're living out here," said Sumi serenely. She craned her neck, grinning at Antsy. "Hello, Trinket. You here to give an answer?"

"It's still my fault," said Emily. "If I hadn't tried to bring it up in the cafeteria, Angela wouldn't have heard me. That was what gave her the idea!"

"And we're getting off topic, which is a neat trick when we haven't even managed to get on topic yet," said Kade. He rubbed his face with one hand as he moved to sit on his own pile of books. "I swear, if I ever figure out how I turned out the responsible one, I'm going to start setting fires for fun."

"You stayed," said Sumi. "Long and long and long enough that I don't think anyone but Elly-Eleanor remembers a time when you weren't here, and maybe even she doesn't remember anymore. And when things got bad, you didn't run or hide, you *helped*. And then you helped again when my daughter showed up, remember?"

"What?" squeaked Antsy.

"I'll explain later," said Cora, putting a hand on her shoulder and guiding her toward a seat. "It's a long story."

"So you helped and helped and you stayed and stayed, and you were steady and sturdy and not hollowed out by hope like the rest of us, and eventually that meant we all started to depend on you to be here when we needed you." Sumi rolled her shoulders in a gesture that would have been a shrug if she hadn't been vertical and contorted. "You're like caramel that way."

"No one, and I do mean *no one,* ask her what she means, or we'll be here all night," said Kade. "Where the hell's Christopher?"

"He was in the library with me, but he didn't come out," said Antsy. "He's supposed to catch up."

"Meaning he's trying to head off Angela and Seraphina, so they don't either come crash this party *or* go wake my aunt," said Kade.

Antsy straightened, suddenly alarmed. "Is Seraphina going to make him bring her here?"

"She can't," said Sumi airily. "He's immune."

"What?"

"Christopher traveled to a world of dancing skeletons, and fell in love with their princess," said Kade. "He calls her the Skeleton Girl, and swears one day he's going to go back to marry her. Which doesn't sound like fun to me, since marriage in her world involves flensing the non-skeletal spouse, but what do I know?"

"Since you're still carrying a torch for a ghostie-girl who's never coming back and doesn't believe in the pleasures of the flesh, I'd say not too much," said Sumi.

Kade blushed. Antsy shook her head, looking at Cora.

"Have you considered handing out orientation sheets before you drag people into whatever sort of club this is?" she asked. "Nothing too involved. Just a little list of all the weird in-jokes and inexplicable references."

Cora laughed. "No, but maybe we should look into writing one."

The door at the base of the stairs slammed. A moment later, Christopher called, "It's just me!"

"What took you so long?" Kade called back.

"Seraphina was real determined to get her hands on Antsy, and you know how much she hates that I don't do whatever she tells me to," said Christopher, as he climbed the stairs to join the rest of them. "She told Angela to go and wake Eleanor, and I had to convince the pair that Cora'd taken Antsy outside. They probably *will* wake Eleanor as soon as they crawl out of the turtle pond—"

"You *didn't*," said Cora, with delighted horror.

"—and even if they decide not to, they're almost certainly going to tell the rest of the school. How do you think the student body reacts to the news that they could go home right now, if Antsy were just willing to find their doors?" He had his flute in one hand, as he almost always did. He looked down at it as he spoke, letting his fingers play gently across the surface. In a softer voice, he asked, "How are we *supposed* to react?"

"The same way we have been, we're just going to have to do

it faster," said Kade firmly. He turned to Antsy. "Please don't think we've only been friendly because we wanted something. You seem genuinely nice, if a little spacy, and we're all spacy while we're readjusting to this world's rules. We figured you'd need friends. But Sumi and I sat down with all the records we've been able to scrounge together so far, and we figured out that your 'I can find anything' was probably literal. Meaning you could find people's doors."

"I can only find a Door while it exists, though, and not every Door exists all the time," said Antsy. "If a Door doesn't exist right now, I won't be able to find it for anybody, not even for myself."

"That's still a lot of doors," said Kade. "You could find them. You could open them."

"I could, but I won't, and you're saying it wrong," said Antsy, frowning deeply. "Everyone here says it wrong, all the time."

"How should we say it, then?" asked Emily.

"Like it matters. Like it means something. Like it's so important that it's worth what it costs." Antsy shook her head. "I can't explain. You either hear it or you can't. But the Doors deserve respect, and caution, and I don't care how many people ask me, I'm not finding Doors for everyone at this school. It wouldn't be right. The Doors don't throw people out willy-nilly. They want to make sure no one gets trapped in something they want right *now* but that's going to eat them alive if they stay there too long. If you're meant to find your Door, you'll find it. I'm not a magic shortcut."

"Even if Seraphina asks you to?" asked Sumi. She rolled onto her stomach, nearly falling off her tower of books, and looked at Antsy with sharp interest. "Even if they come weeping and begging at your feet, please, please, just let me go home? They won't care about shortcuts or whether it's 'meant to be.' People never do. They'll only and ever care that you *could* help them, you *could* release them, but you don't."

"Don't you want the same thing?"

"Me? Nah." Sumi shrugged. "I know I go back. When the time's right. I'm not in any hurry to push the issue. I want to give Confection as much time as it needs to make sure the present and the future are happening in the right order, and not wind up when I'm not supposed to be. Ponder doesn't need to be *that* much older than I am, and I don't need a kid who's already had more birthdays than me running around."

"Right, Confection," said Antsy. "Time happens there in whatever order the world needs it to, except when something really important happens."

"I have to save the world," said Sumi. "Defeat the Queen of Cakes once and for all, and usher in a boring ol' age of heroes." She whipped the ribbon off her fingers, untangling it instantly, and waved it above her head like a banner. "Whee."

"You know about Confection?" asked Kade, ignoring Sumi as he focused on Antsy.

Antsy froze.

Finally, she said, "I know a lot of places."

6 THE LONG WAY HOME

"I DON'T KNOW *ALL* the places you've been—I could never go to any of the Drowned Worlds, it wouldn't have worked out very well for me, since I breathe air and all the ways we had of fixing that were too permanent to be safe—but I know *of* most of them." She paused for a moment, noticing how raptly they were all watching her. "Did you know Seraphina probably went to a Drowned World?"

"She didn't," scoffed Cora. "I would know. That girl's dry as a desert."

"Oh, I figure she went to Auxesia, and it's a split world. Dry above, wet below. They live on ships the size of cities, and they fight war after war to own the most beautiful things in the whole world." Antsy looked at the piles of books around them. Much easier than looking at the people. "When they can't find something beautiful to fight over, they make it. So they lure pretty girls through Doors, and they . . . pearlize them, sort of. Make them the most beautiful things that ever were."

"It's always girls," said Kade, with an odd sort of bitterness. "What happens to the girls they take?"

"Um. Most of them die, which is why I wasn't allowed to go there. Some escape into the sea, and become water-people, and then they don't worry as much about being beautiful. But most of them never come home." Antsy glanced back down the stairs. "I wonder why Seraphina did."

"Because she's awful," said Cora. "Probably even a whole

world full of awful people figured out they didn't want her there."

"A better question might be why she wants to go *back*," said Emily. "Sounds like a bad party to me."

"And when Emily and I were talking in the cafeteria the other day, she said something about maple syrup being the 'blood of the divine,' so I'm pretty sure she went to Harvest."

Emily sat up straighter, eyes suddenly very bright, fingers digging into the floor.

"Do you think the children who travel from different parts of the world use so many English words to talk about the places they go?" asked Sumi.

"No," said Antsy. "The worlds have their own languages."

Everyone, even Kade, stared at her.

"Explain," he said.

Antsy blinked. "Um. It wouldn't make sense for all these different places to develop the exact same ways of talking? But no one ever goes through a Door and finds themselves totally unable to talk to anybody around them. The Doors give us language when they give us passage, and take it back when we pass through again. So what you call 'the Trenches' is actually called," and she made a strange, harmonious warbling sound that was something like whale song and something like a word that was designed to be heard across miles of open water.

Cora paled and swayed, grabbing the top of the banister to steady herself. "Never do that again," she said to Antsy.

"Um. Sorry," said Antsy. "It's just, it matters, because when people have tried to find other ways to travel, they didn't get the words, and so they got really lost."

"There are other ways to travel?" asked Christopher.

"Stop pressuring her," said Emily. She stood, smooth and graceful, and moved to offer Antsy her hand. "It's okay, kiddo. Come sit with me."

Antsy gave her a grateful look and took the offered hand, letting herself be led.

"Kiddo?" asked Cora. "Em, she's the same age we are."

"She's not, though. Look at the way she stands, or the way she's so careful and precise when she uses really big words. You remember Rowena."

Cora and Sumi both made sounds of dismay. Emily looked to Kade and Christopher.

"Ro was one of our dorm mates at Whitethorn. She was the same age we were—or so we thought. But she'd been to a world made of clocks and time, and it ate up her whole childhood. She was six when she went. She was twelve when she came back, three hours later. She'd been at Whitethorn for five years. She stayed behind when we ran." She glanced at Antsy. "She hid it well, but she used to get the same trapped look in her eyes that Antsy does, when we were talking about things she was still mentally too young to understand. How old are you, Antsy?"

No one had asked her that, not once, not even Eleanor, and so it was probably unsurprising when Antsy started to cry. She pressed her face against Emily's arm as the other girl stroked her hair, and when she finally felt like she could speak without her voice breaking, she sat up, wiped her eyes, and said, "I'm nine."

"Antoinette Ricci—you're that girl whose stepfather murdered her!" said Christopher, snapping his fingers. "I mean, I guess not, but it was all over the news a few years ago. They never found a body. I was in the hospital for chemotherapy when it happened. I saw a lot more breaking news than I wanted to."

"Is that what they say he did to me?" asked Antsy. "I saw my mom—she thought I was someone else—and she said he was in prison, but not why. She said something about pictures . . ."

"And if you don't know, we're not going to tell you, because you shouldn't have to know that," said Kade firmly. "I remember that story too. I'm sorry, Antsy. Why didn't you say something?"

"Because I missed being around other people," said Antsy. "People my actual age would think it was weird if a teenager wanted to hang around them all the time, just like you'd think it was weird if someone who looked nine wanted to hang around you all the time, so it seemed best to keep my mouth shut."

"Your world did this to you?" asked Cora.

Antsy pressed her lips into a thin line and shook her head. Then, more slowly, she nodded. "Yes," she said. "And no. The world didn't. The world is . . . The Place Where the Lost Things Go is neutral. Most Nexus worlds are. All of its magic goes into sorting and cataloging, and maintaining the Store."

"You talk about them like they're two different places," said Emily.

"Because they are. You don't talk about your bedroom and Ohio like they're the same place, even if your bedroom's *in* Ohio. The Place is the world, and the Store is where travelers end up. I think maybe the Store is the actual Nexus."

"You said we should talk about the doors—sorry, the Doors—like they were important enough to be worth what they cost," said Kade. "What did you mean?"

Antsy hesitated. Finally, looking at her knees, she said, "Every time you open a Door, there's a toll. It costs. I don't know exactly how much, because it doesn't take money, and it doesn't tell you. You probably wouldn't even notice unless it happened a whole bunch of times, over and over and over again."

Emily gasped. The others turned to her, attention attracted by the sudden sound. She sat up straighter, refusing to wilt under the combined weight of their gazes, and said, "Time. That's what they take. That's why Antsy looks so much older than she is. The doors take time."

Antsy nodded. "I opened a *lot* of Doors," she said, in a small voice.

Emily put an arm around her shoulders, suddenly protective. They made an odd tableau, the pale, skinny girl with the wild red hair and the body language of a wounded animal and the dark-skinned girl with the meticulous braids, holding Antsy close like she wanted to fight the world on her behalf.

"No one's going to make you open any more, I promise," she said. "We want to go home, but you're not our skeleton key."

Christopher made a choked noise.

Emily's attention swung to him, expression silently questioning.

"I'm sorry," he said. "I'm not trying to say Antsy should . . . It's just that the term 'skeleton key' has some pretty bad associations at this school. A former student went on a murder spree not that long ago, trying to make one for herself."

"I was a victim!" said Sumi cheerfully, raising her right hand to make a V sign next to her temple.

"What?" asked Emily.

Someone started knocking on the attic door. Christopher sighed. "Guess they got out of the turtle pond," he said.

"Now what?" asked Cora.

"We could thump 'em!" said Sumi.

"The only one of us who'd be able to keep swinging once Seraphina was actually in the room is Christopher, and since she'd just make the rest of us gang up on him, that wouldn't work," said Kade.

"This is why I hate making plans," said Sumi. "They always fall apart."

"This was a good plan," said Cora. "Find out whether Antsy could actually locate people's doors, and talk to her about it *privately*. We just forgot that Seraphina pays attention to gossip, and puts things together remarkably quickly sometimes."

"Plan didn't account for her being the one to figure it out for sure," said Kade. "That's on me. We were trying to figure out how we'd bring this up to Eleanor when Seraphina went and forced the issue. All right, Christopher. I've got some laundry sacks over there. Go ahead and grab one."

"Why?" asked Christopher, already moving to do as he'd been told.

"Because you're going to put it over Seraphina's head before the rest of us can see her."

Christopher stared at him. "You're *joking*. That's not a solution. That's a comedy routine."

"Well, Lundy was the one who knew how to reflect that damned gaze of hers back on her, and she's dead now, so we don't have much better!" snapped Kade. The knocking on the door below was getting louder. It was beginning to verge on pounding. There were other voices in the hall now, students lured out of their room by the ruckus and pressed into the ongoing assault on the attic door. "Aw, screw this. I'm calling my aunt."

He got up and began digging through the books behind him, looking for his cellphone.

Antsy pulled away from Emily as she stood and stared off into the attic. "Or I could just get us out of here before she breaks the door down," she said.

"Antsy?" asked Emily.

Antsy barely heard her through the rising static, the sudden ringing in her ears. After a long pause, broken by the hammering on the door, she nodded.

"I can afford one," she said. "All of you, follow me. It only charges the person who does the opening. You can follow, as long as you don't let the Door close, and if you let it close, it's probably going to disappear."

If any of them replied, either to accede or object, she didn't hear it. She was already wandering deeper into Kade's sanctuary, slipping between towering stacks of books and into a narrow aisle defined by heaped-up bolts of fabric. She didn't bump or brush against anything. In fact, as she walked, she began to relax, feeling more at home than she had since leaving the Store. The Doors may have taken her childhood to pay for passage—and while she feared and respected them, she didn't blame them; no, that was reserved for the adults who failed her, the ones who refused to tell her what they knew when it might have helped—but the Store had kept her safe. It had protected her from her stepfather, it had given her a purpose and a home, and she missed the narrow, towering shelves more than she could say.

Kade's attic was a return to the familiar. She couldn't hear the others stumbling after her through the ringing in her ears, but she did see Kade dart forward to catch a box of trim that one of them had somehow dislodged, before it could come crashing down and hit her. She shot him a grateful look, and kept going.

A hand grabbed her arm. She shook it off. The attic was large, but even large rooms can't go on forever, and the wall was just ahead, dust-brown wood visible between shelves and piles of sewing supplies, and the outline of a door etched into the planking. There was no drywall, no attempt to disguise the wood, just faded stain, worn with age, but the Door was clear.

It had been formed by small discolorations in the wood itself, by scratches from moving furniture and old irregularities in the stain. It would have been easy to overlook, if it hadn't been shouting quite so loudly. At the very top of it, the woodgrain swirled in tight, almost regular loops, becoming words:

Be Sure.

"I am sure I can afford to pay three days for the sake of not becoming Seraphina's lapdog," said Antsy, voice clear and calm. Then she reached for the illusion of a doorknob.

It was no shock when her hand closed, not on empty air but on a crystalline orb, and the door blossomed into existence in front of them.

It was an imposing, rainbow-hued thing, seemingly carved from a single pane of shimmering crystal. There was no direct light on the door, but it sparkled all the same, as glittery and alluring as anything had ever been.

The ringing stopped. Antsy looked over her shoulder. The others were staring at her. Kade, particularly, was paler than she was, which was odd, given his normally golden-brown complexion.

"Are you sure?" asked Antsy.

The pounding below them stopped as the attic door slammed open.

"Yes!" shouted Emily.

Antsy opened the door.

PART II

GETTING LOST AGAIN

7 INTO THE GLITTER HELLSCAPE

ANTSY HELD THE DOOR open as the others tumbled through, moving so quickly that Christopher tripped Kade, who stumbled and landed on top of Cora, causing her feet to slide out from underneath her. She sat down, heavily, on the glistening hillside.

"Oh, Lord, I am so sorry—" said Kade, pushing himself away from her and grabbing Christopher's arm as he got to his feet. "Are you hurt?"

"No," said Cora. "But where *are* we? Antsy?"

"This isn't one of the worlds I've visited," said Antsy. She looked around.

Most of the others were doing the same—all except Kade and Sumi. Kade was looking fixedly at Cora, and Sumi was watching Kade, standing with the easy readiness of a warrior who thought she might be called upon to start cracking skulls at any moment.

They had appeared on a gently sloping hillside, the kind that was almost an invitation to stretch out in the grass and just start rolling. The grass itself was lush and emerald green, but gleamed with rainbows where the light hit it. A forest grew above them, trees close together without becoming foreboding, and those, too, glittered like their leaves had been painted in streaks of impossible color. Tiny rainbow flowers dotted the hillside, and the sky was alight with sheets of dancing light, like the aurora borealis had decided to appear during the day and everywhere.

"It's beautiful," said Cora, whose peacock-blue hair had a similar oil-slick nacre to it.

"I think I'm going to be sick," said Kade.

"It's Prism, and we should leave as fast as we can," said Sumi.

Christopher swore.

Emily looked confused. "Why? Is it dangerous?"

"This is the world Kade's door took him to," said Christopher. "The one that threw him out because he wasn't what they expected."

"Why did you open *this* door, Antsy?" asked Cora. "Why not any other?"

"I told you, I can only find a Door while it exists, and this was the closest one that would get us out of there," said Antsy frantically. "I wasn't looking for Kade's Door, or anyone's, specifically. I was looking for a way out. Is this a Fairyland? It feels like a Fairyland."

"It is," said Kade, voice gone dull. "And like all Fairylands, it has rules, and it doesn't like when people break them, even accidentally. I can't be here. They didn't throw me out because I wasn't sure. They threw me out because I *was* sure, and I *am* sure. This is a paradise if you're exactly what it wants you to be, and the first person who ever saw me clearly was from here, and he's dead because I helped the people who hate me kill him."

"Do you know *roughly* what it costs to open a door?" Emily asked, anxiously.

"Three days, I think," said Antsy.

"Do you have to open it?" asked Sumi. "Or can you just find it, and leave it for someone else?"

"I . . . I just have to find it, but you may not be able to open it if it's entirely inimical to you as a person," said Antsy.

"Guess Jill should have waited awhile to start up with the snicker-snack," said Sumi. "We found a skeleton key after all, and if she'd just been a little patient, she'd be an undead monstrosity by now, instead of a puzzlebox girl spread out across a thousand surgeries." Then she laughed, magpie-bright, and moved closer to Kade. She set a hand on his arm.

"Hey," she said, voice gentler than Antsy had realized Sumi's voice could be. "The door wasn't there because you have any obligations left to these people, or this world. It was there because sometimes people can't let go of who they thought we were, and so they keep trying to tangle us in nets and drag us back. That doesn't mean we have to go. Or if we do go, that doesn't mean we have to *stay*."

Kade looked at her, tears running down his cheeks. "I just . . . I loved it here so much, Sumi. So, so much. It was perfect. Everything here was perfect, except for me, and so they made me leave instead of changing enough to let me be perfect, too."

"People who can't change aren't really perfect, and no matter how much we love it somewhere, that doesn't mean it's good for us," said Sumi. "You have to listen to me. I *died,* and that means I'm clever now." She looked over her shoulder at Antsy. "We *can't* stay here. Find another door. Doesn't matter where it goes. But don't you open it! I was dead for *ages,* and came back same as I ever was. I can afford to spend a few of the days I didn't get to use the regular way on getting us away from here before somebody notices we've arrived."

"I'll try," said Antsy. She turned a slow circle, eyes half-closed, head cocked like she was listening for something. When she returned to the place where she started, she opened her eyes and shook her head. "I'm sorry. There isn't one right now."

"Not even back to the school?" asked Kade, a thin edge of panic in his voice.

"Not here," said Antsy. She wrapped her arms around herself, visibly frustrated. "I don't know how close something has to be before I can find it. I didn't find the school, even though I needed to be there, until after I found my mom and also Angela's kitten."

"So maybe we just need to move," said Emily, trying to sound encouraging. "That's all. Come on, let's go. Kade, is it safer to head for the trees or down toward the base of the hill?"

"Trees are goblin territory," said Kade distantly. "Dangerous for the Courts. Open ground is best for them. Branches catch and tear fairy wings."

"So we're heading for the trees," said Sumi. "Come along, Kade, you can tell me what mushrooms not to eat."

Kade stirred himself, focusing on Sumi for the first time. "All of them," he said. "*All* of the mushrooms are not for eating. Sumi—"

She was already laughing and skipping away, and Kade had to hurry to catch up with her, leaving the rest of them to walk more slowly behind. Christopher fingered his flute as he walked, but was the first of them to put into words why they weren't rushing, as long as Kade and Sumi were in sight.

"Kade would tell us if we were in danger while the fairies aren't around. He's never said anything about Prism being one of those worlds where the grass tries to eat you or anything."

The others glanced nervously at their feet, which continued to move normally, no roots or vines catching hold of them.

"Not that he talks about Prism much," said Cora.

"Am I allowed to ask what happened?" asked Emily.

Christopher glanced ahead, checking Kade and Sumi's location, then said, in a low voice, "Prism's a Fairyland, and like Kade said, Fairylands get real hung up on rules. One of the rules of Prism is that they only take girls from our world. I know all the doors mostly catch girls, but Prism does it on purpose."

"Auxesia is the same way," said Antsy.

"So when they grabbed Kade, they thought they were getting a girl to fight their battles, and when they discovered their mistake, they kicked him to the curb. He's been at the school ever since." Christopher shrugged. "Most of us want to go back. Want to go *home*. Kade never has. That's why this feels sort of like a mean trick."

"It wasn't," said Antsy. "I wouldn't. It's not."

"I know. But you can see why he might be a little upset, right? Being forced to go back to the one place in all the worlds that he never wanted to be again?"

Antsy nodded, expression miserable, and kept walking. Emily slowed to stay even with her.

"Hey," she said. "You didn't do anything wrong, okay? We needed a door to get us out of there, and you found the only one available. We'd be doing whatever Seraphina wanted right now if it weren't for you. Like finishing her math homework, or filing her nasty toenails." Emily wrinkled her nose in an expression of exaggerated disgust.

Antsy giggled.

"So see, you helped a lot more than you may have accidentally hurt. If you need to, you can say sorry. If Kade says he doesn't want to talk about it, you don't. The way you fix things now is by finding another door. It doesn't have to belong to any of us." Emily's expression turned a little wistful. "Maybe it's better if it doesn't."

"Don't you want to go back to Harvest? You talked about it like you did."

"Oh, I do. More than anything else there is. More than dancing, even—not that I could dance at a professional level now, not after my time at Whitethorn."

"They hurt you?"

"Absolutely yes. Everything they did to us was meant to do us harm, and they were very good at what they did. If you mean physically, then no. That would have been too obvious. It was still a school, after all, even if it was a school run by the bad sort of monsters. What they did to me . . . they wouldn't let me dance, Antsy. Ballet is what I love more than anything else in *this* world, and I'd been in lessons since almost the time I could walk. The last doctor who looked me over said that my legs and hips will never be free of pain, because of the amount of ballet I did, and it was worth it, or it would have been, if they'd let me keep training so I could be good enough to dance professionally." Emily sighed. "But now, I'll never be anything more than a talented amateur, because while I was at Whitethorn, they took away my dancing—*all* my dancing, even the kind that doesn't need training at all. I had to do my exercises in the space between the beds when no one was watching, just to stay limber enough to hold on to hope."

"Harvest likes the people to dance," said Antsy.

Emily nodded. "Exactly. If they'd managed to break me to the point where I couldn't bring myself to dance at all, I would never have been able to go home."

"So why don't you want me to find your Door?"

"Because I'm not sure yet." The admission seemed to pain her. "I wanted to ask if you *could,* because I hoped if I knew you *could,* I'd finally be sure enough to make it come back for me. I didn't want you to actually do it. I missed my family while I was over there. I missed my ballet classes, and reality television, and my cat." She laughed, high and unsteady. "Well, my family sent me to Whitethorn, and they gave away my cat while I was gone, and ballet isn't the same now that I know I'll never be as good as I could have been. So I guess I just love reality television so much that I'm never *sure.*"

"Everyone has something," said Cora, who had slowed to walk just barely ahead of them, Christopher still ahead of her. Perhaps twenty yards farther up the hill, Sumi and Kade were stepping into the shadows of the trees. "It doesn't matter what it is. If it's yours, it's enough."

In the distance, a hunting horn blew loud and long, and ahead of them, Kade shouted, "Come on, get to the trees! They're coming!"

Emily took Antsy's hand, and they broke into a run, Cora ahead of them, Christopher stopping at the edge of the wood to look back and be sure they didn't leave anyone behind. Sumi emerged from the trees, darting forward to grab Christopher by the shoulders and yank him into the woods, like some sort of strange but efficient predator.

Nothing grabbed or tripped or stopped the rest of them, and in no time at all, they were reunited in the safety of the trees, the horns still ringing in the distance, the sunlight slanting through the prismatic leaves.

"Now what?" asked Christopher.

No one seemed to have an answer.

8 SOME FLOWERS BLOOM IN SHADOW

"I DON'T KNOW," said Kade, when the horns stopped and the silence stretched so thin that it felt like a breath would break it. "I've never spent much time in the woods."

"Too bad Regan's not here," said Sumi, who had already made her way halfway up a tree. She was straddling a branch, tapping a spray of shelf fungus with one fingertip. Every time she touched them, they cycled through another color, like a very slow, very silent rave. "She's good at forests."

"I am not," said Cora. "Lakes, sure. Oceans, awesome. Forests, no, thank you."

"Better here than Confection," said Christopher.

Cora shuddered. "Oceans should *not* be strawberry soda."

The silenced horns were replaced by the pounding of hooves and the jingling of tack. Cora reached out and took Kade's hand. All of them, even Sumi, stared at the forest's edge.

"Should we run?" asked Antsy.

"No. We're in the trees. They won't see us, and even if they do, they won't take us. There are rules." Kade said the last word like it was bitter in his mouth, all but spitting it out.

"So we stand," said Sumi, dropping out of the tree and taking Kade's other hand.

They kept watching the edge of the wood.

A company of tall, brightly dressed figures on horseback rode up to the edge of the woods. Their horses gleamed with mother-of-pearl, white, black, gray, and roan. Their tack was polished silver, and their clothes were elegant and flowing, somehow combining dozens of disparate shades without clashing at all.

As to the people themselves, they had long, flowing hair and equally long, beautifully patterned butterfly wings which sprouted from their shoulders, slowly fanning the air.

Antsy stared. Sumi scoffed, looking like she was about to say something, but stopped as Christopher motioned her to silence. Kade clung to Cora and Sumi's hands like he was in danger of drowning if he let them go.

"Well?" asked the lead rider, in a voice like sharpened ice.

"Nothing, Majesty," said another. "There was no Door. There is no traveler. Or if there were, they have already gone to the Goblin Wood, and we shall not see them again."

"Not before the battlefield," said the first. "Very well, then. Another failure. Must all Doors be disappointments?"

"It seems this is not an age of heroes," said yet another rider, and they turned, as one company, to canter away into the distance.

Kade started breathing again.

"I do not know *how* I ever thought those stuck-up, vicious *assholes* were wonderful," he said. "I should have seen right through them."

"You were a kid," said Sumi.

"Still."

"When I was a kid, I thought broccoli wasn't poisonous."

"Sumi . . ." Kade shook his head. "Never mind, there's no point. Got a Door yet, Antsy?"

"I'm not sure." Antsy closed her eyes.

The ringing in her ears started almost immediately. "This way!" she said, opening her eyes as she pointed deeper into the forest. She bounced onto her toes, beaming. "There's a Door this way."

"Can you tell where it goes?" asked Cora.

"Not until I see it, and maybe not even then," said Antsy. "I'd never been here before. I could have guessed 'Fairyland, probably,' but not 'Prism.'"

"Let's go," said Kade. "We'll be quick and quiet, and hopefully we're out of here before anyone else sees us."

"But you said—"

"Goblins," said Kade, and started walking.

The others followed. Antsy quickly took the lead, and the others followed, trusting her to find the best way to the door that only she knew was there to find.

Less light made it through the branches overhead, although what light there was remained full of rainbows. More fungus appeared, glowing when Sumi touched it, although she obeyed Kade's injunction against sampling the stuff, no matter how bright and candy-like it seemed. Finally, they approached a small cave, the walls lined with geode spikes.

Antsy bit her lip. "We have to go in there," she said.

"I would prefer not to," said Cora stiffly. "That's pretty narrow."

"It's the only Door I can find right now," said Antsy. "I don't know how often they appear without being used. We could go back to the woods and wait, I guess, if Kade says it would be safe . . ."

"It wouldn't," said Kade. "The longer we're here, the more chance the goblins realize someone's in their territory and come looking. The last time they saw me, I was standing over the body of their king, and I'm the reason he was dead on the ground. They're not likely to be very glad to have me here."

"You looked really different then, though," said Christopher. "Maybe they wouldn't recognize you."

"Magic," said Kade. "They'd know me."

"'Maybe' is a hook to catch the unwary," said Sumi. "Maybe it's going to be better tomorrow. Maybe the snake won't bite. Maybe the mushroom won't be poisonous *this* time. If Kade says it's not safe to stay, we listen to him, same way we'd listen to you if we went to Mariposa."

"Fine," said Cora. "But if I get stuck, you're all going to have to help get me out, and not one of you will ever say a word about it again."

"There are trees here," said Sumi. "I bet I could make syrup."

"Isn't syrup sticky?" asked Antsy. "That seems like the opposite of what we want."

"Not if I ask it not to be," said Sumi.

Kade sighed, and was about to say something else when he abruptly stiffened, eyes going wide. "Into the cave," he snapped, tone leaving no room for argument. Antsy moved almost without intending to, ducking into the narrow tunnel, Christopher and Emily close behind.

Cora came after them, moving with the delicate care of someone who knew her environment was not on her side, but who had become resigned to the risk it offered her. She held her breath as she inched her way in, concentrating to avoid the crystals lining the walls.

Outside, Sumi grabbed Kade by the hand and tugged him toward the cave. He stayed where he was, staring off into nothing.

"Hey," she said, voice low and sharp. "Hey, tailor-boy, you need to come with me now."

"I killed the king," he said. "I did it. I didn't know what I was doing, or why it was so wrong, or why I didn't want to hurt him, but I did it anyway to please the Queen, and he's dead because of me. If they catch me, they'll punish me for what I did." He turned to look at Sumi, tears bright in his eyes. "It doesn't matter that I was just a kid who thought he was doing the right thing. It doesn't matter that they lied to me. I did it. Shouldn't I pay for what I did?"

"If we all paid for everything we'd done, there'd be nothing left in all the worlds but debtors' prisons." Sumi yanked on his hand again. "We're your penance, silly, the whole chaotic bunch of us, and as part of your penance, I say you're not done suffering us yet. You have to come and keep paying before you're allowed to go and get your head chopped off for the sins of your past. Now come *on*."

She pulled a third time, harder, and this time Kade started moving, letting her yank him into the cave. The others were well ahead of them by now, and despite her concerns, Cora didn't appear to have gotten stuck.

Sumi was moving fast, and pulling Kade in her wake. They caught up with the rest of the group in a small, crystal-lined chamber filled with a pale golden light that came from the walls themselves, cast in crystal. Kade exhaled, slow and shaky. Christopher turned to look at him.

"You okay, buddy?"

"We weren't supposed to go into the caves, because they were goblin territory," said Kade. "But I did it anyway. They were the only place in the whole world that hadn't been written in rainbow, and sometimes I just wanted to see things for one color at a time, the way they really were."

"Ooooo . . . kay . . ." said Christopher. "Going to take that as a yes."

Antsy, meanwhile, was staring at one of the chamber walls, trembling slightly. Emily put a hand on her shoulder.

"Antsy?"

"It's mine," said Antsy. "Can't you see it? You could all see the Door to Prism in the attic."

"There's something that could be an outline, I guess," said Emily dubiously. "Why are you so scared?"

"Because it's mine, and because I *am* sure. It feels different than Kade's did. It's not hunting. This Door doesn't hunt on this world. It's here because it wants me back," said Antsy. She stumbled as Sumi pushed forward, shouldering her to the side. "Hey!"

"Touch the door so the rest of us can see it, and I'll open it up," said Sumi. "I told you I'd pay to get us out of here. I have the time banked from when I was busy being dead."

"If you're sure . . ."

"I'm ridiculous, not indecisive," said Sumi. "And unlike Eleanor, I'm not afraid of growing up. Confection wants me no matter when I am."

"All right," said Antsy, and reached out, and touched a spire with the tip of her index finger.

It was like a screen had been whisked away. There was no transformation or ripple in the world: it was simply a crystal spike before she touched it, and a plain brass doorknob that could have been found in any ordinary home after she did, round and smooth and slightly tarnished. There was no point to having a doorknob without a door, and so of course a door came with it, wood painted white and ordinary as anything, with a bronze sign hanging at exactly Antsy's eye level.

ANTHONY & SONS, TRINKETS AND TREASURES, it read, and below that, in smaller but bolder letters, so that they would be impossible to miss: BE SURE.

"I'm always sure," said Sumi, and opened the door.

9 FILED AND FORGOTTEN

THE DOOR FOUGHT SUMI as she opened it, but she was strong, muscles densely packed under the layer of softness she had cultivated with candy and cakes, and in the end, she won, yanking the door open to reveal what looked like the back room of a thrift store as big as a warehouse. Things were piled in every direction and on every surface, haphazard and threatening to come tumbling down in great cascades of other people's junk. The smell of aging paper and fabric that had been stored for too long without being worn wafted out to greet them.

"Well, go on," said Sumi, breaking the silence.

"The Store," breathed Antsy, and stepped through, face alight with wonder and joy, both tempered by wariness and loss. Emily was close behind her, stepping daintily between the piles on the floor. Christopher went next, pausing to turn back and offer his hand to Cora, who rolled her eyes as she took it, letting go as soon as she was through the door.

Sumi looked to Kade. "Time to go, unless you've changed your mind about wanting to stay," she said. "I still say we're a better punishment for your crimes than decapitation or whatever weird penance the goblins would come up with, but it's your call."

"I never wanted to come back," said Kade. "If it's allowed at all, it feels like it's something that should be the whole point, not something that happens almost by accident when no one's looking. This isn't my world, not really. It was hers, and she never existed anyway, and so I'm not staying here." He moved past Sumi, pausing before he stepped through the door to kiss her forehead and murmur, more quietly, "Thank you."

Sumi laughed and waved him away. "Go-go-go. I'm going to be a married woman, so there's no point to pining over me, not with Ponder already waiting."

Kade smiled back, then moved into the store, following the others.

Alone in the cave, Sumi exhaled. "All right," she said. "You can come out now."

Silence filled the air. Sumi continued to look straight ahead, watching the others move deeper into the store.

Finally, a voice behind her said, "You let the Opener go on without you."

"True enough."

"We could overpower you. Close the door. Strand you here without your friends."

"I guess you could, if you wanted to be meanies to someone you haven't even met yet."

"Aren't you afraid?"

Sumi smiled. She was still facing front, but anyone behind her would have seen the way her cheeks pulled up, the way her shoulders relaxed.

"Nah," she said. "If you wanted someone to be afraid, you should have tried to menace somebody other'n me. Maybe it's logical of me and that makes it a bad idea, maybe it's me being irrational in the face of a system that doesn't work the way I want it to, but I know my door's coming, and Confection doesn't care where I am when it decides to take me home. It found me in a place where no one else's doors could find them, and it let me leave again, because it wasn't time yet. So you can strand me here for a while, but you can't keep me forever. Say what you came to say, leave, and let me go."

"Was that truly our prince?"

"According to him, yes, no, and maybe. Your king named him prince as he was dying, but then the fairies kicked him out of Prism, and he doesn't want to come back here because he'd have to deal with them. And maybe he'll change his mind and maybe he won't, but it's his mind to change and his choice to make. Does that answer your question?"

"Tell him we miss him."

Sumi scoffed. "You never *knew* him. The fairies had him the whole time he was here, and you left him in their care."

"We knew him on the battlefield. He fought like a lion, even when he was so young that our warriors feared to raise blade against him, lest they be condemned for cutting down a child. He was never cruel, but would not yield to those of lesser skill. He was made for this world. This world was made for him. We regret his absence."

"I could say a lot of things, and most of them would be true, and all of them would be cruel, so I'm not going to do that right now. I'll just say I'll pass your message along, and I can't do that if you don't let me leave."

"So we have an agreement."

"No. We have an understanding."

Still not turning to the goblin or goblins that had come up behind her, Sumi stepped through the door. It swung shut, and when she did look back over her shoulder, there was no door there, only a long corridor shaped by shelving, stretching off into the dimly lit distance.

"Huh," she said. "That was kind of annoying."

She faced front again, intending to go after the rest of

the group, and stumbled backward, arms pinwheeling frantically, as she found herself suddenly face-to-face with Emily.

"Ack!" said Sumi.

Emily recoiled, and Sumi landed on her bottom in a heap of vinyl records and manilla folders full of ancient tax returns.

"I'm sorry!" said Emily.

"You startled me," said Sumi. "I'm impressed." She reached up, waiting for Emily to pull her off the floor, and when the other girl didn't move, lifted her eyebrows in silent question. "Well?"

"I came back because we were worried about you," said Emily, taking her hand and hoisting her to her feet. "Antsy was afraid the door might have closed before you could come through."

"Oh, no, nothing like that." Sumi waved her free hand idly. "Just taking care of some loose ends. Where are we? Did Antsy say for sure?"

"Oh. Um, yes. This is the Shop Where the Lost Things Go. Antsy's door, like she said before you opened it for her. Thank you for that, by the way. After Rowena . . . I understand why she's so afraid of her body being older than it's supposed to be. I guess we should have realized they'd take something from us, when they were giving us so much. I was just so busy focusing on what I had, and then on what I'd lost, that I never stopped to think about it."

"None of us did," said Sumi. "I don't much care for reading—if I read a page and then you read it later, we'll both see the words in the same order, unless one of us is dyslexic, but most people will see it the same, and that's too logical for me. Even so, when I first came to the school, when I was so scared that this was it, I was never going to see Ponder, or swim in the strawberry sea, or go gathering fallen konpeito during the star showers ever again, I read everything there was about the doors. Most of it Eleanor wrote herself, but Kade edited it later, so it would make sense to more linear people. I read Eleanor's original text. And none of it, ever, said anything about a toll. I guess because even people like Elly-Eleanor only get to go through five or ten times, and that's a month, maybe. Not enough to notice."

"Antsy is trying to find the front counter," said Emily. "She says the Store is aware enough to only offer you what it wants to, and if it doesn't want her to find the counter, she won't. Being able to find anything she's looking for started when she left here, so maybe it doesn't work anymore."

"Huh," said Sumi. She pulled her hand free of Emily's, cupped her palms around her mouth, and shouted, "*Hello the Store!*"

Her voice echoed through the rafters, booming off into the distance, where it lost all texture and definition and seemed to become nothing more than the simple sound of thunder.

Sumi dropped her hands. "Huh," she said again. "Big place. Guessing you could look for something in here for a long, long time and not find it if it didn't want to be found."

"Yeah," said Emily, giving her a perplexed look. Voices and footsteps hurried toward them through the shelves, and a moment later, Antsy came around the corner, the rest of the group behind them.

"Sumi!" said Christopher, hurrying forward. "Girl, you scared us halfway to death. I thought we'd lost you."

"I'm a bad penny," said Sumi. "I always turn up, even when you halfway wish I wouldn't. Have you been having a grand adventure in the universe's junk shop?"

"Mostly we've been following Antsy around and watching

her get lost, which is novel enough to be almost entertaining," said Cora. "Also, I found the friendship bracelet my second-grade bestie made for me before her family moved to Florida. I lost it that same summer."

"Stay here long enough, you might find your second-grade bestie, isn't that right, Antsy?" asked Sumi.

Antsy looked uncomfortable. "People don't usually wind up here. People are smart enough that they don't get lost very much without intending to, and someone losing track of you doesn't mean *you're* what got lost. It normally means what got lost was caring about what the people looking for you think."

"What a fascinating and convoluted cosmology you must live with here, said the girl made of literal living gingerbread who exists in an asynchronous timeline. How fun it must be to think about at night."

"You don't have to be mean," said Antsy.

"Sadly, sometimes, I do," said Sumi. "If I was nice all the time, that would be predictable, and if I become predictable, I die inside."

"Do you think the store is hiding the front desk from you?" asked Cora. "Why would it do that?"

"I think it's hiding the people I'll find there from me, and it's doing that because it doesn't want me to yell at them the way I did the last time I was here," said Antsy.

Emily frowned. "Why did you yell?"

"Because they've been lying to kids and letting them get hurt when they didn't have to, and it's not fair and it's not right and it's not the way this place should be." Antsy shook her head, eyes bright with anger and conviction. "This is a good place. It's a necessary place. It's a nexus, the same as Earth; almost all the Doors can open here, even if they can't on every world there is. Lost things from all over everywhere wind up here, and sometimes people come to find them, and sometimes people come because they need something only we can give them."

"This is normally where there's a catch," said Christopher.

"There are so many Doors here that it's almost impossible to resist them, and they cost so much more than you realize when you start, and the people who should be warning the newcomers about the toll aren't doing it," said Antsy. "They didn't have to do that. They didn't have to lie, or hide things. The Store knows that, or it wouldn't have let me learn it."

"But it's protecting those people?" asked Christopher.

"It could be."

"I don't like that at all," he said. "There might be something I can do. Hang on just a second."

And he raised his bone flute to his lips, and he began to play. Or to pantomime playing: only Sumi smiled and swayed along to the music none of the rest of them could hear. And in the dust under the shelves, something rustled.

Antsy gave a little scream and jumped back as skeleton mice and beetle shells began creeping into the open, moving on legs that had no flesh remaining, waving broken, dust-covered antennae.

Christopher lowered his flute, smiling.

"You said *people* didn't tend to get lost unless they meant to," he said. "These weren't people. They were small and they got swept up into the wrong places, but they weren't people. And some of them died here. You can find mice and beetles in every shop in the world, even the very cleanest. They're part of this place now. Even if it doesn't want you to find the front desk, they'll be able to show us the way."

"Really?" Antsy looked to the tiny scattering of skeletons and chitin on the floor. "Can you show us to the front desk?"

The skeletons made no sound, but bobbed their assorted heads in what looked like agreement before turning to scamper down the aisle, in the opposite direction of whatever Antsy had been leading them toward. Christopher raised his flute and started playing again.

More tiny creatures emerged to join their strange procession. Emily smiled as a pair of skeleton mice ran over her shoe.

"Just like home," she said.

They kept walking.

The aisle gave way to another, almost identical aisle, which gave way to a series of shorter aisles filled with bookshelves, followed by a long corridor of dish hutches, each filled with mismatched dinner sets and chipped wineglasses. This corridor, at last, opened into a wide space, open enough for them to all gather together rather than walking single file. Three sides of it were surrounded by more of the endless maze of shelving. The fourth was dominated by a long, time-worn wooden counter with an old-fashioned register on one end and a well-lit employee area visible behind it. A stairway to an unseen second floor rose to one side, the steps stacked with more items, like even in this infinity of shelves, there could never be enough.

A small bronze bell rested there, next to a perch that looked like it was designed for some sort of large parrot. Only Antsy seemed to take any notice of it.

The rest of them were busy staring at the doors.

They seemed to appear on every possible surface, on walls, on shelves, sometimes without any surface at all. A few would have been accessible only by ladder, or by someone who already knew how to fly. Others were freestanding, doorframes appearing in the middle of an aisle. They came in an endless array of styles and colors, with knobs of polished metal, crystal, and petrified bone. One even had a large, living rose where a doorknob should have been, yet somehow there was no question that it was a door: anyone could have turned the knob and stepped through.

Anyone.

Antsy ignored them, walking stiff-legged toward the counter and slamming her hand down on the bell so hard that the ringer bit into her flesh. A tinny chime rang through the area.

No one came to answer it.

"Service!" she yelled. "I have come through a valid door to the Store Where the Lost Things Go, and I demand service as a customer!"

Something rustled at the top of the stairs. Emily and Cora wrenched their eyes away from the doors—for Emily, a door made of sticks and straw, through which flickers of firelight could be seen; for Cora, a door that seemed to have been made from woven kelp, which rippled and pulsed with the endless motion of the sea—and turned toward the rustling.

A child, no more than six or seven, ran down the stairs. She wore a dress of patchworked gingham, like something out of a fairy tale, and her hair was pulled into messy pigtails much like Sumi's, save for the fact that they were tied with mismatched ribbons instead of licorice ropes. Her feet were bare, and there were two small white scars on the side of her neck that telegraphed her world of origin as loudly as any announcement, at least to those who had been to the Moors. Cora shivered and turned away.

"Sorry, sorry!" said the girl, voice bright and quick and

suited to her steps. She flung herself behind the register, then turned toward Antsy, small face glowing with the eagerness to be of service. "Hello I'm Yulia, welcome to the Store Where the Lost Things Go, how may I help you today?"

It came out almost as one long word, rushed and rattled off, but clear and perfect all the same. Yulia glowed with pride, even as Antsy looked at her with horror.

"Where are Hudson and Vineta?" she asked, voice going shrill. "Why are you alone here? *How old are you?*"

The last question that seemed to matter the most, because she stared at Yulia after it was asked, waiting for an answer. Yulia looked uncomfortably around the group of teens, then back to Antsy, before she said, in an uncertain tone, "I'm . . . five? At my last birthday, I was five. That's when the Master took my sister to be one of his daughters."

She started to cry then, overwhelmed as any child would be by a group of strangers staring and shouting at her. The curtain behind the counter rustled and was drawn aside as an ancient woman in a long silk dressing gown stepped out, leaning heavily on a walking stick as she fixed her rheumy eyes on Antsy.

"Just because the Store decided your services were no longer needed, that doesn't give you the authority to yell at your replacement," she said, voice stiff and sharp and commanding.

Listening to it, Kade could easily see why a confused child would accept this woman as an immediate authority. *He* half-wanted to accept her as an authority, and he was nowhere near the age of the trembling Yulia, or even the righteously furious Antsy.

"The Store let me leave because I wasn't sure that people who'd spent my childhood like someone else's coins had the right to keep me," said Antsy, voice icy. "If it didn't want me here, it didn't have to let me come back. None of my companions are suitable employees. You look like you've aged a few years in my absence, Vineta. Couldn't resist when you didn't have a convenient child to exploit?"

Vineta stiffened. "You have no right to come into my home and talk to me like that," she spat.

"And you have no right to stand behind that counter telling lies to children, but here we are." Antsy continued to glare at her. "Elodina's spirit remained in this place long past when she should have been allowed to rest, because the Store needed *someone* to do what you refused to do. Someone had to warn them, had to warn *us*, before we followed you to the grave."

"Age is a fair trade for experience," said Vineta.

"This isn't the Goblin Market," countered Antsy. "Not everything is about fair value. And is it really fair value if you don't understand what you're paying? I opened one Door to get us here. One of my companions opened another. We both knew the price before we paid it." She turned to Yulia. "Did she ever tell you what it costs to open a Door?"

The smaller girl sniffled, but had not yet started to cry. "I don't have any money," she said. "And I don't have any *things* apart from what I'm wearing. But I still have all the blood in my veins, and all my memories of my sister are sunlit ones. That's enough for me. If the Doors cost something to open, it's a good exchange for comfort and safety and a full stomach and no vampires scratching at the windowpanes begging our mother to let them come home."

"See?" Vineta smiled at Antsy, triumphant. "Yulia understands a good trade when she sees one. She knows this is the right place for her."

"She is a *child*," said Antsy.

"So are you."

"Not anymore!" Antsy spread her arms wide, making it impossible to miss the height of her, the obvious age of her. "I'm a teenager, and I won't ever get to be a child again, and I didn't get to be a child the first time. If I want to do childish things, or be with other kids, I'll be judged for being weird, or being threatening, or being scary, because you took the time when I should have been allowed to play and turned it into something else. You turned it into trying to survive, to serve the adults around me, and you didn't care if it was hurting me, because it wasn't hurting *you*. As long as it wasn't hurting someone who mattered, you didn't care."

"No one warned me. Why are you owed anything different?"

Antsy shook her head. "Just because someone hurt you when you were a child, that doesn't make it right for you to hurt anyone else."

"Says the girl who dragged a legion of the door-touched to the land of their deepest desires." Vineta turned her attention to the rest of the group. "She told you what this place was, didn't she? Did she also tell you not to pick forbidden fruits?"

"She did," said Kade.

Vineta continued anyway: "This is a Nexus. Worlds that have the strength to open Doors will open them here, as well as on whatever world waits on the other side. The travelers who reach this place can use it to move from world to world, with intent. With *purpose*. Doors that open here don't require a perfect match the way they do when they open elsewhere. There's no need to be sure. No need to be ideal. She could open Doors for every one of you, and send you onward to your heart's desire, whether what you yearn for is your original destination, or another. Have you always yearned for a world someone else described to you? She could get you there, and as you would have come through a universal door, your conviction would have no power to eject you."

"We already knew that she could find Doors before we came here," said Emily, stepping forward, so that her arm was just brushing against Antsy's. A show of support, a reassurance through presence. "She also told us what it costs to open them. I'm sorry, ma'am, and I was taught not to speak rudely to my elders, but I have no interest in someone else paying my debts. If Harvest wants to call me home, it'll come for me when the time is right, and if it doesn't, then I suppose it was never really home to begin with."

"That's a very indecisive way to plan a future," said Vineta.

"Maybe, but it's mine, and I know what I want. If the doors know our hearts enough to seek us out in the first place, I suppose Harvest's going to know my heart well enough to know when to let me come back."

"No support here, angry lady who steals from kids," said Sumi.

Vineta wrinkled her nose. "You stink of gingerbread."

"*Big* insult. Was that one hard to come up with?" Sumi sounded genuinely curious. "I was born on Earth—all of us were, I think—and I died there, so they re-baked me on Confection. Dying was dull, though I gave it a whirl. You can't catch me. I'm the Gingerbread Girl." Then she laughed, as wild and unashamed as ever.

Antsy, meanwhile, had taken Vineta's distraction as an opportunity to move closer to Yulia and crouch, putting herself somewhat on a level with the younger girl. "Hey," she said. "I'm Antoinette. I'm from a place called Earth, and I had your job for a long time."

Yulia eyed her warily. "You can't have it back, it's mine now."

"I don't want it back. I just want you to understand what you're giving up by doing it."

Yulia's wariness melted into pure confusion. "I'm not giving up anything."

"But you are. Every time you open a Door for her, you pay three days of your life. If you open ten Doors, that's a whole month." Yulia didn't look like she understood, so Antsy tried again, saying, "They're making you older."

"I *want* to be older," said Yulia.

"Didn't you want to be all grown up when you first came here?" asked Vineta, apparently done trying to understand Sumi. "You lied about your age, told us you were older than you were, because you couldn't wait to be adult and free to make your own decisions. Well, we only gave you what you wanted. We enabled you to grow up quickly, in a safe place, where the people who'd hurt you couldn't hurt you anymore. That's what the Store gives its clerks. Safety to grow up. The few like you who choose to leave, they go back to their worlds too adult for their tormentors to touch."

"I wanted to be grown up because I didn't understand what that meant!" cried Antsy. "I didn't know it would mean my mother wouldn't recognize me, or that I wouldn't be able to ever, ever, ever go home!"

Vineta looked at her coldly. "It wasn't our job to explain that to you."

"But it was. You were the adult. You needed to tell me what would happen if I stayed here and opened doors for you, you needed to make me *understand*. You didn't have to be my enemy, especially not when I thought you were my friend."

"Bah." Vineta turned away from her. "The Store dismissed you. Your services are no longer needed. We're fully staffed, and you may go. Open your own door, or take three days off the child; either way, you're not welcome here."

Antsy's hands opened and closed, flexing furiously with the visible urge to strike the old woman. Kade stepped forward, putting a hand on her shoulder and half-turning her to face him.

"Hey," he said. "What's the goal here? What did you hope would happen?"

"Before I left, I told them we had to start making sure the children who came here understood what the doors would cost them, and that they knew they'd grow up too fast if they were careless about the how many they opened. You can still open doors; you just need to be selective about it, not go opening them willy-nilly because you can." She gestured to Vineta. "*She* likes novelty. She likes to go shopping in new places and taste new foods, but she's almost out of time, and she can't open the doors the way she used to. She needs someone else to do it for her. So she tells the kids who come here that they have to do it on her behalf. That it's normal."

Antsy's glare was hot enough to burn. "She speaks for the Store, and she doesn't tell us what any of this costs. The Store *used* to tell the children, but somewhere along the way, that stopped, and now all of us who come here do it without knowing what we're being asked to give up so adults can live easier lives. Anything that's lost anywhere else can wind up here. Anything that's lost here is lost forever."

"And you hoped . . . ?"

"I hoped I'd find that they'd listened, and started doing the right thing, and I could go back to Earth and figure out how to be happy where I came from." Tears started rolling down Antsy's cheeks. "But they didn't. They're still hurting kids, and now I have to stay here, even though I can't open any more doors without hurting myself, to make sure they *stop*."

"You keep saying 'they.' There's only one person here. Antsy, who else are you talking about?"

"Hudson. He's the magpie who keeps the books balanced and tracks the inventory. There aren't any humans who came from this world originally, just magpies, but all the magpies everywhere came from here." Antsy looked around, remembering the bird's absence for the first time since she yelled at Yulia about it. "He should have come when I rang the bell. He has wings, so he should have come faster than the people."

"The big black bird?" asked Yulia.

Antsy nodded.

"Miss Vineta said he was a busybody who told lies, so we put him away."

"Put him away where?" asked Antsy, stiffening.

"She put him in a cage, and I opened up a Door, and then he was gone away, poof, no more feathers, no more lies."

"And once a Door is closed, it's gone," said Vineta, with a certain degree of cruel satisfaction. "Bye-bye, birdie. Aw, are you going to cry because you can't force me out?"

"He was your *friend*!"

"He was my employee, and he was spying for the birds who think they own this place." Vineta crossed her arms. "I know how much time I have. I know how many Doors I can—or can't—open, and I know I'm not going to let myself be forced out of my home by some feathered scold or his shrill sycophant. You'll never find him. And you'll never

convince Yulia that you know what she needs better than
I do."

Antsy whirled and stalked away, back into the shelves,
leaving her friends behind her.

10 FRIENDS OF A FEATHER

"YOU ARE NOT A very nice person," said Cora, voice firm and angry, before she turned and hurried after Antsy. Christopher was only a step or so behind.

"A *cage*?" asked Emily, before she ran after the others.

Kade didn't say anything, just looked at Vineta witheringly and followed the group.

Sumi, left alone with the old woman and the little girl, produced a piece of ribbon from inside her pocket and began winding it through her fingers, creating an intricate loop. Vineta sniffed.

"What? Aren't you going to judge me too? Don't you have some cutting comment to make you feel better about coming here, to my home, and judging me by your own standards?"

"Nope," said Sumi.

"Then why are you still here?"

"Because I figure you were like Antsy once, and like Yulia here. You were a kid who fell through a door trying to get away from something that wanted to hurt her, and you thought you'd stumbled into paradise." She kept twining and twisting the ribbon between her fingers, looping it joint by joint. "And somewhere along the way, you figured out paradise was pay-to-play, but you'd already paid so much that you couldn't dream of stopping. There was nothing else for you. Nowhere to go, no one to turn to, no way out. Time to make the best of a bad situation, since there's no way of making anything else."

Sumi looked at Vineta with cool, unnerving eyes.

"You're not wrong," said the woman. "But that doesn't give you the right to—"

"People who've been hurt often think they have some sort of right to go around hurting other people," said Sumi. "They think trauma's a toy to keep handing down forever. But the fact that someone hurt you and tied you up in knots doesn't give you the right to do it to anybody else. I'm a formerly dead girl made of gingerbread and hope, and even I can see that." She tugged one end of the looped and knotted ribbon, and it came free of her fingers, untangled, untied. She stepped over and offered it to Yulia, eyes still on Vineta.

"I hope you can figure that out one of these days," she said. "Or no one's going to remember you kindly, or care when you're gone, not really."

Yulia reached out and tugged the ribbon from Sumi's hand, looking bewildered.

Sumi flashed her a quick, tight smile. Then she turned and skipped after the others, pigtails bouncing in time with the rest of her.

Vineta scowled and snatched the ribbon out of Yulia's hand. "They won't be back," she said, with calm certainty. "Spoiled children have to learn they can't have everything they want. You understand that, don't you, Yulia?"

Yulia nodded, making no attempt to hide her confusion. Vineta sighed.

"Let's go pick another door," she said. "It's time to figure out what we're doing for lunch."

Among the shelves, Antsy and her friends moved deeper into the store, Antsy stomping, the others just trying to keep up. Kade kept glancing back, until he saw the top of Sumi's head appear briefly over a short shelf and relaxed. When she caught up with the rest of them, he reached over and swatted her companionably on the shoulder.

"Stop letting yourself get left behind," he said. "You're bad for my nerves."

"Stop leaving me behind," she said, tone prim. "I'm great for my own amusement."

"Maybe don't squabble right now?" asked Christopher. "Antsy's worried about her friend."

"*Is* the bird her friend, though?" asked Sumi. "Only because it sounds like he's one of the people she's mad at."

"You can be mad at your friends," said Cora. "I've been mad at most of my friends at one point or another. I was mad at Nadya, when she left me behind in the hopes of getting back to Belyyreka. I knew it was the right thing to do, because we'd never have gotten Sumi back if she hadn't gone, but I was furious with her."

"Nadya—that was the little Russian girl with an arm made of water that no one could see, right?" asked Sumi.

"Yes, Sumi," said Cora. "She stayed in the Halls of the Dead so they'd let us take your ghost with us when we went to Confection."

"So many people, coming and going, to-ing and fro-ing, where does it all end?" asked Sumi.

"When I find the Door that takes us to Hudson, and we hope he's still alive," said Antsy hotly. "The Doors appear here whenever they want to—I don't know what draws them, or if they show up in time with something from the other side getting lost enough to wind up in our intake pile, or what, and I was never able to figure out a pattern reliable enough to tell me what was coming—but before I left the Store, I didn't find things on purpose, I just *found* them. I guess the Store making me leave made me figure out how to do consciously what I'd been doing all along."

"Meaning you think you can find a specific Door now?" Emily looked back over her shoulder. "Vineta said that once a Door was closed, it was gone for good."

"Yes. It is." Antsy glanced at her. "A Door is a passage. You don't take the same Door into and out of a world. They disappear every time you close them. Where she's wrong is in thinking that another Door won't open to the same place. I *do* think I can find specific places, or at least find *Hudson*. Putting him through a Door to a world he doesn't know—putting him in a *cage* . . . that's maybe the worst thing I've ever heard of someone doing to another person."

"Apart from murder," chirped Sumi. The others turned to look at her. She blinked at them. "What? I didn't much like it when Jill murdered me."

Antsy reached the end of the aisle and turned sharply left, heading along the shelves toward a corner. The store had been bigger than this a moment ago, hadn't it? Could it really be rearranging itself to get them where it wanted them to go? Maybe. If it was, maybe that meant it was on Antsy's side, not Vineta's.

It was something to hope for, at least, and she hoped all the harder when they reached the corner to find two tall doors waiting for them. One was painted in colorful funhouse red and blue; the other was roughhewn, barely shaped enough to be considered a door at all, rather than a naturally occurring pile of sticks and branches.

"They didn't used to advertise what they were this clearly," said Antsy. "Most of them looked like the ordinary doors back at home, like they were trying to be ambushes. Now

I can see exactly what they are, and if either of these led to a world I'd been to visit before, I'd be able to just look and know it."

"How do we know which one to open?" asked Sumi. "Do we each take one, or . . . ?"

"This one's mine to pay for," said Antsy. "I left him alone with her, even if I didn't mean to. I should have realized there was no way she'd stop, and that it didn't matter how many threats I made if I wasn't here to enforce them. So this one's on me."

"Aw, but I was looking forward to chasing my birthday around the calendar."

Antsy stepped between the two doors and closed her eyes, raising her hands until her palms were pointed toward them, the funhouse on the left, the woodpile on the right.

"Clowns," she said, after a moment's long silence. "Greasepaint and sawdust and the sound of screams and laughter, and maybe they're different things, but maybe they're not always. Darkness, and a terrible logic, and Hudson isn't there." Her shoulders sagged with what looked like relief. "That's not the right door. The other one . . ." Again the pause, again the silence, before: "Green leaves and rain and the sound of storms. Teeth and claws and running, but no malice at all. Just nature, doing what nature does. Nature, and *Hudson.*"

Opening her eyes, Antsy turned toward the woodpile door. "This way," she said.

She stepped forward, grasping a particularly protruding branch, and pulled the door toward herself. There was a moment of resistance where it seemed jammed into the frame, unwilling to be moved, and then, with a low creak, it swung open, and revealed the world beyond.

At first it seemed like they were looking at the densest

rainforest jungle that had ever existed, all towering trees with broad green leaves, dangling vines, and bell-shaped flowers larger than Antsy's entire head. The ground was a sea of tall ferns and unfamiliar brush, with nothing resembling grass in any direction. Small creatures rushed and rustled through the growth, sending everything moving constantly in different, irregular directions.

There was no sign of a birdcage, or a black-and-white bird, but Antsy looked pleased all the same.

"This is the one," she said. "She put Hudson here. Someone needs to stay behind."

"Why?" asked Sumi.

"I can prop the door open to keep it from closing while we're on the other side, which is important—if it closes, it disappears, and I have to spend another week or two of my life bringing us back here the long way. I've never had a doorstop get knocked loose before, but . . ."

"But you've never had Vineta out to get you before, either," said Kade, somewhat grimly. "I don't want to let y'all out of my sight, you know that, right?"

"I'll stay," said Christopher. They all turned to look at him. He shrugged, grimacing apologetically. "Whoever's world that is, it's completely antithetical to mine. That's so alive it hurts my eyes. I want clean bone and cultivated flowers, not wild growth and rotting. I'd only slow the rest of you down."

"Thank you, Christopher," said Antsy, and reached for a box, using it to prop the door open before she stepped through. Sticking her head back into the Store, she said, "You don't let this Door close for *anything,* you understand me? Not for *anything.*"

"Yes, ma'am," said Christopher.

One by one the others followed her through, into the endless green, until Christopher was left alone. He watched them talking, Antsy pointing off into the distance, and then they plunged deeper into the ferns and tall brush, until he wasn't looking at anyone at all.

Christopher sat down, flute in his hands, and settled in to wait.

11 THE GLORY OF THE GREEN

SUMI SNIFFED THE AIR as they walked. "Ever spend much time in the reptile house at the zoo?" she asked.

"I don't like snakes," said Emily.

"Not on purpose," said Kade.

"Some," said Cora. "Especially after I got back from the Trenches. It was dark and cool, and if I sat on one of the benches and closed my eyes, I could pretend I was underwater."

"That's what it smells like here," said Sumi. "Reptile house."

She wasn't wrong. There was a primal, *primeval* smell hanging in the air, heavy and dense, like someone was wandering around spraying snake-scented perfume directly from the bottle all around them. Antsy blinked.

"I hadn't thought of it that way."

"Does that mean there are big, hungry lizards around here?" asked Emily. "Because I'm really not in the mood to meet a big, hungry lizard. Or a big, well-fed lizard, honestly. If I can just register an anti-lizard position with the court now, that would be a real time-saver."

"Uh, don't think that's gonna work so good, Em," said Kade, looking down at something by his feet. The others moved to see what he had found.

A footprint, pressed into the earth, talons and toes and the broad spade of the sole all stamped into the soft ground. In a few hundred years, under the right conditions, it would be the sort of fossil track that drew tourists from all over, if this world ever developed tourists. In the here and now, it was half-filled with water, and occupied by a frog that watched them warily, clearly suspicious of their intentions, and yet entirely unafraid.

Kade looked up. "I have always wanted to say this," he said, and took a deep breath before saying, in a sonorous voice, "*Welcome,* to Jurassic Park."

Nothing charged out of the trees to devour them as punishment for his irreverence, thankfully. Emily and Cora laughed. Sumi and Antsy looked unimpressed.

Kade sighed. "No one appreciates the classics anymore," he said, as they kept walking.

The edge of the jungle loomed closer and closer. "The Doors tend to open near some sort of market or other population center, since the Store mostly uses them to restock things people don't lose as much," said Antsy. "So maybe you come out near a bakery, or a sandwich shop, or something, just so we can bring back food for the employees. Food that people lose normally isn't anything that somebody would want to *eat.*"

"I don't see any grocery stores around here," said Kade.

"So there's probably fruit or something we can gather in the trees," said Antsy. "Anything that grabbed Hudson's cage would probably have run this way to crack it open and eat him, and he could have flown up into the branches."

"Or something could have gobbled him up," suggested Sumi. The others turned to look at her with varying degrees of horror and disbelief. Only Kade looked unsurprised, even fond, as if this were exactly what he would expect from her. She shrugged broadly. "What? You were all thinking it. I just put it out into the open where you'd all have to look at it instead of walking along trying not to believe it into being."

"Sumi . . ." said Cora.

"Not wanting to look at a thing doesn't make it not so; it just makes it so the thing can lurk and loom and leap out when you don't expect it. If you want a life without terrible surprises, you should always look at the worst possible answer until you understand it all the way down to the bottom. Once you can do that, you'll know what's coming, even if you'll never learn to like it."

They kept walking. Some of the ferns reached to their waists—which meant, in Sumi's case, that they reached all the way to the top of her arms—making it look like they were wading through an endless river of feathered green. While they still saw the ripples through the brush, those ripples seemed to be avoiding them, making it even more obvious that they were watching the movement of small animals. Despite the lack of ripples close by, the ones only a little farther out were no more frantic than the rest; they were being avoided, not fled from.

"I don't think anything here is afraid of us," said Emily. "Why isn't anything here afraid of us?"

"Because I think Kade may have been right about where we are. I mean, without the venture capitalists perverting the laws of science and nature for the sake of making a few bucks, that is," said Cora. "I don't think humans are a thing in this world yet, if they're ever going to be. I think this is the age of dinosaurs."

"That would explain the smell," chirped Sumi.

Emily's shoulders dipped, face relaxing like she was allowing herself to have a thought that she'd been pushing aside before. "How many worlds that belong entirely to dinosaurs do you think there are?"

"Not too many that we can get to from the Store," said

Antsy. "They'd have to be safe enough for us to access, and have something—anything—that we could use. Which is why I'm guessing there's edible fruit somewhere up ahead."

"That's what I hoped you would say," said Emily, and stopped walking. Placing the tips of her pinky fingers side by side in her mouth, she whistled high and shrill, the sound echoing across the green field and into the forest beyond before it faded. Something in the distance roared, a deep, primeval sound that sent shivers up their backs. The rest of them stopped walking in turn, looking at her.

"What was that for?" asked Kade.

"Emily . . ." said Antsy.

"I think I know what she was doing," said Cora.

Something in the forest whistled back, just as loud and just as long, and Emily lit up like a birthday cake, eyes so bright there might as well have been candles lit behind them.

"Stephanie," she said, and broke into a run.

Not wanting to be left behind or to lose track of her in this strange place, her companions ran after her, Cora and Sumi keeping pace with ease, while Kade and Antsy lagged behind. The whistle from the trees came again; Emily was too busy running to whistle back.

Then they were charging into the dimness under the first level of the jungle canopy, and a ghost was dropping down from the branches to meet them.

Antsy was pale, the kind of white that looked like paper next to most people; all her color was in her freckles, and it had been that way for as long as she could remember. Cora was a few shades darker, with a greenish tan that was still technically within the human range of skin tones, although it was pushing the absolute limits of what that term could mean. Sumi, Kade, and Christopher were varying shades of pale to medium brown, while Emily was the darkest of the group, with deep brown skin that seemed almost the polar opposite of Antsy's . . . at least until the ghost appeared.

This girl—for it was a girl, about Kade's age, tall and slender and delicate, as long as one didn't focus on the visible muscles of her thighs or shoulders, which were sharply defined and spoke to a life of constant physical effort—was so pale that she seemed to glow in the shadows, too white to be real. If Emily was anyone's opposite, it was hers. It didn't help that the girl's hair was the same color: platinum blonde, short and ragged, as if she had been cutting it with the wicked-looking bone knife that hung at her belt.

She was dressed in a tunic of sorts, made from what looked like pebbled alligator hide, red with bands of gold. The sides were held together with sinew knots, and her belt was braided strips of shed reptile skin. Her feet were bare.

"Emily!" she squealed, and the two girls crashed into one another in a tight embrace.

"Holy what the hell is going on here?" asked Kade.

"Emily whistled and called a ghost out of the trees and the ghost is really pretty and doesn't need to share a dorm with me anymore and I'm going to seduce her," said Sumi.

Kade gave her a sidelong look. She shrugged.

"What? It's better to be upfront about these things when you can. Makes it more surprising when you can't."

Emily and the ghost had let each other go, and the ghost was turning to Cora, beaming. "Hi, Cora," she said.

"Hi, Steph," said Cora. "This is your dinosaur world, huh?"

"Uh-huh. I don't know if it has a name—the locals aren't big on naming things just yet—so I call it Rodinia, after the supercontinent before Pangaea. Maybe they'll call it some-

thing else someday, when my bones are in one of their muse-
ums, frightening children, or maybe they'll never get that far.
Maybe the comet comes tomorrow, and my bones are used
by Creationists to try to sell the idea of some all-powerful
god. I'm dead either way, so I don't much care."

"Dead here?" asked Emily.

Stephanie nodded, pale blue eyes solemn. "Yes, dead here.
I'm sure. I was sure when Sumi found me that door on
Confection—hi, Sumi, we'll talk about that seduction comment in a little bit, after you tell me what you're all doing
here—and I've stayed sure ever since. I was only unsure the
first time because I hadn't said goodbye to my parents. Well,
they packed me off to Whitethorn, so now I'm sure I don't
owe them anything. Try to conversion-therapy me into someone I'm not, see if I ever do anything nice for you ever again."

"So you're staying," said Cora. "Won't you get lonely?"

"What? Why would I get— Oh. You think just because
there's no mammals here, I'm all by myself. Well, that's not
true at all." Stephanie turned around, put her fingers in her
mouth, and whistled, a different tone than the one she'd used
to answer Emily.

Something in the jungle answered her, a high, inquisitive
trill.

"Everyone be very, very still, and stay quiet," she said, just
as the first tall figure emerged from the brush and started
toward them.

"I am going to punch Michael Crichton in the mouth so
hard," said Sumi, voice awed.

"He's dead," said Cora.

"Just means he won't fight back."

The creatures approaching through the foliage shared a
shape with Crichton's velociraptors, being tall, long-tailed

raptor-type dinosaurs. That was where the resemblance stopped.

Their bodies were covered in iridescent feathers as filled with rainbows as the skies of Prism or the oil-slick sheen of Cora's hair, deep jewel tones shifting with every motion of their bodies. They moved like birds did, heads remaining steady even as they bobbed at the end of long, sinuous necks. Their lower legs, upper arms, and lips were bare and scaled, exposing teeth and talons, but there was a bright intelligence in their amber eyes. They knew and understood the world around them.

The largest moved to stand next to Stephanie, bumping her shoulder with the tip of its snout and making an inquisitive warbling sound. Stephanie warbled back, then rubbed the top of the dinosaur's feathered head, looking back to the cluster of humans.

"This is my family now," she said. "They don't care that I don't have feathers, or that I make weird noises and smell strange. I've learned enough of their language for us to communicate, and they're glad I'm here with them. They're my family, and they love me."

The dinosaur bumped her shoulder again.

"They're afraid I'll go with you, since I vanished once before, and I think that for *this* world, I'm the start of stories about children falling through doors." She laughed. "I get to be the foundation of a myth! How sick is that?"

"Pretty cool," agreed Kade, sounding bewildered.

Emily, who had been Stephanie's roommate longer than either Cora or Sumi, who had been there during the desperate flight from Whitethorn, looked at her gravely. "You're sure, then. This is still what you want?"

"As if I didn't seem sure enough when I left you all in

Candyland so I could go home to my family, where I belonged?" Stephanie spread her arms. "There's no electricity
here. No running water, no modern medicine, no internet.
No grocery store or coffee. And I have never been happier.
This is where I *belong.*"

"Sometimes the Doors get it right when they go fishing
for children," said Antsy. "We didn't come to take you away."

Stephanie relaxed, looking pleased and—obscurely—just
a bit disappointed, like she'd been expecting something else.
"Oh. Why did you come? I know you didn't find a door.
Emily would be miserable in a world that hasn't invented
Halloween yet, and Cora would hate the ocean here. It's full
of giant lizards made of teeth, and they're *not* as smart or
friendly as my family."

"What about me?" asked Sumi.

"Refined sugar doesn't exist."

Sumi's eyes went wide. "This is hell. We've discovered an
Underworld for certain, because this is hell, and everything
that happens here is designed for torture and for torment."

"We came," said Antsy, forcibly ignoring Sumi's theatrics,
"because we're looking for a magpie who was shoved into
a birdcage against his will. A black-and-white bird, named
Hudson. He's very talkative, and I'm sure you'd remember
him if you'd seen him."

Several of Stephanie's dinosaur relations stepped forward,
lips drawing back from their teeth as they began snarling.
The feathers atop their heads rose in what was clearly a threat
display. Any question of whether feathers would make dinosaurs *less* terrifying was promptly answered. No. No, these
literal living dinosaurs with their literal mouths full of sharp,
pointy teeth were not any less terrifying just because they

were also brightly colored and a little fluffy. If anything, the contrast made it worse.

As for Stephanie, she tensed, stance shifting to something defensive. "Hudson? What do you want with Hudson?"

"Please," said Antsy. "He deserves to go home, and he can't open Doors on his own."

"Says the girl who stuffed him into a cage and threw him into the bushes in a world full of predators! If Two-Chirps hadn't found him, he'd have been eaten."

"*I* didn't do that!" protested Antsy. "Vineta did. Yulia said Vineta called him a liar who lies, and that means he was trying to tell her what the Doors charge for using them, and Vineta didn't want her to listen. He was probably also trying to tell Vineta to stay away from the Doors before she ran out of time completely, and *she* didn't want to listen to *that*. So she got rid of him. But now I'm back, and I'm not leaving the Store again, and I need his help so I can get rid of *her*."

Something rustled overhead, and then a voice asked, "Truly?"

Antsy exhaled, shoulders sagging. "Truly," she repeated. "Hello, Hudson."

With a flurry of wings, a large black-and-white bird dropped down from the branches and landed on the ground at Stephanie's feet. Unlike the dinosaurs, who wore neither clothes nor ornamentation, the bird was wearing a tiny pair of wireframed spectacles, shaped to rest on his beak and hooked behind his head to make up for his lack of ears.

"Hello, Antoinette," he replied. "I didn't think I'd see you again."

Antsy laughed, covering her mouth with her hand. "Last time we were together, I yelled at you and stormed away."

"I needed yelling at." He fluffed his feathers. "We made a promise to Elodina. We promised to tell the new clerks what the Doors cost. But it was so much easier to run the Store when we had full use of them, and most featherless people have such long, long lives; Vineta said *she* didn't know, and *she* didn't get upset when she found out, so why should anyone else? And she said if I didn't stop telling lies and asking her to stay away from the Doors, she'd get rid of me." Hudson's wings drooped, his head dipping low in sadness and shame. "I thought we were friends. I thought we both wanted what was best for the Store."

"I don't think she's wanted what's best for the Store for a long time," said Antsy. "I'm going to replace her."

Hudson cocked his head. "You're sure? Because you weren't, or the Store wouldn't have made you leave."

"The Store sent me another promissory Door," said Antsy. "That means I was sure enough to call it back to me. Maybe someday, when it's been long enough and I'm all the way an adult the *right* way, I'll open a door back to my mother, when she can believe I'm really me. Until then, I can resist the Doors, and I don't mind letting other people open them if they understand what it's going to cost. We can ask customers to open a Door for us if we tell them it'll cost them three days off their lives, and we can keep taking care of the lost things, and actually be a *safe* place for the children who find us, instead of a trap that pretends it's a safe place all for the sake of doing them more harm."

"Do you understand any of this?" Stephanie asked, looking to Emily.

Emily smiled. "Some of it. I understand that Antsy's going home, and not coming back to school with us."

"School?" Stephanie took a step back, toward the safety of

her watchful, vigilant dinosaur family. "Did you go back to Whitethorn?"

"No, no, to the other school, the one Sumi told me about." Emily sighed, still smiling. "They let me make scarecrows for the garden out back, and sometimes I go out there to dance at night. It's beautiful."

"She's a wonderful dancer," said Cora. "Hardly ever steps on a single snail."

"Snails have a right to exist as much as we do," said Emily.

"And the crunch feels weird between your toes," said Sumi. "Hi, Stephanie. Wanna go into the bushes and get nasty?"

"Thanks, but we've been out in the open long enough; it's not safe to stay here."

As if Stephanie had summoned danger by speaking, something deeper in the jungle roared. It was a bone-shaking, primal sound, one that instantly reminded all of them that they were soft and squishy creatures, capable of being killed.

"We should be somewhere else," said Stephanie.

"Roger that," said Kade, and the lot of them fled deeper into the jungle, following the dinosaurs away from the sound of roaring.

12 HAPPY LITTLE TREES

"NOT WHAT YOU EXPECTED when you got out of bed this morning, is it?" asked Kade, panting with the effort of keeping up with Cora. She was always faster than he expected her to be, even though he knew well and good that out of the pair of them, *she* was the athlete. He was happier sitting in his room sewing or working on the Compass, while Cora was like as not running laps around the school or swimming in the turtle pond, a habit which no longer particularly upset the turtles.

"I've learned never to expect anything specific," said Cora. "I *did* expect the day to be a little shorter. It was night when we left, but it's been daylight in every place we've gone with windows. Does your Compass tell us why that is?"

"Nope." Kade looked after Antsy with something like yearning in his expression. "Never had the access or the opportunity to learn."

"Kade . . ." Cora swallowed back a terrible suspicion. "You can't stay at the Store, even if you want to know those things. Eleanor needs you. The school needs you." *I need you,* she thought but didn't say aloud. Her crush was one-sided, and she knew that. Still, Kade's presence did so much to keep the school running as smoothly as it did. Maybe it wasn't fair to put so much on his shoulders when he was still technically a student, but he'd taken most of that weight on willingly, and at this point, too much would collapse without him. Eleanor needed him, both as an assistant and a family member.

Although maybe it was time they start thinking about seriously talking to Eleanor, finding out what responsibilities could be shifted from Kade to other members of the school community who had no intention of leaving after graduation. They needed fewer potential points of failure. Especially since she knew that Eleanor herself was counting the days until her door would open again, and she'd be welcomed back into her land where up was down, down was up, and nothing had to matter more than a moment.

Well, right now, it was the moments that mattered most. Whatever had roared behind them wasn't roaring anymore. Instead, it was pursuing their group through the jungle, every footstep striking the earth with an audible thud that seemed like it should have been shaking them off of their feet. Stephanie and her family were well ahead of the others, familiar with the terrain, using the tree roots and lowest branches as leverage to boost themselves further or as jumping platforms, letting them cover more ground, more quickly.

Sumi and Emily were both behind. They were athletes in their own way, the warrior and the dancer, and they were both fast when they wanted to be. For all Sumi's casual insistence that Confection would call her home when the timeline decided it was ready for her, she still trained, hard, for that day, knowing that once she went back, she'd have to defeat the Queen of Cakes in order to claim the happy ending she believed was waiting. Emily . . . even if she was never going to be a professional ballerina, she still danced, and dancing involved a general level of physical fitness.

Which left Cora pacing Kade, even though she could have gone much faster, so as not to leave him alone.

"I know," he said, glumly. There was a wheezing note in his voice that Cora didn't care for. "I also . . . know . . . that I . . . should join . . . PE class . . . when we . . . get home."

"Yeah, you probably should," she said, and smiled at him as they ran.

One of Stephanie's dinosaurs had doubled back and ran with them, making small sounds of concern that wouldn't have been out of place coming from a giant pigeon. Cora tried to wave it off.

"We're good," she said. "Just slow."

The dinosaur made a disapproving noise. Cora managed, barely, not to laugh at the ridiculousness of the whole situation, and focused on running instead, just as the beast that had been chasing them burst out of the trees.

Kade suddenly found a burst of speed that he'd previously been unable to access, and raced on ahead of them, leaving Cora blinking after him.

"Coward," she muttered, and glanced back.

The beast was another dinosaur, that much was obvious, but one built on a much larger scale. Stephanie's family was made up of predators, no question; with their teeth and talons, they couldn't have been anything else. This one, however, was at least ten times their size, and had only patches of feathers around its neck and at the end of its long, thick tail, like ornamentation more than plumage. She might have called it something akin to a *Tyrannosaurus rex,* only a monster example of its kind, and also chasing her.

The dinosaur that had come back to check on her slowed, putting itself between her and the terror, and roared its own challenge, feathers puffing out until it was almost spherical. Cora kept running. She felt bad for doing that, but she hadn't asked the dinosaur to endanger itself, and she wasn't going to waste the time it might have bought her.

The others were up ahead—she could still see them, and she'd been holding back to run with Kade. While none of them could possibly outpace the monster dinosaur for long, she could at least speed up until she felt the burning in her lungs.

The smaller dinosaur popped back up, running beside her. "Glad . . . you . . . didn't . . . get . . . eaten," Cora gasped, feeling slightly more sympathy for Kade's earlier lack of air.

Not much, though.

Up ahead of them, the others had disappeared. That was a little alarming. Cora kept running. The pair entered a clearing, and the dinosaur darted ahead, stopping at the mouth of what looked like a hollowed-out log tilting downward into the unseen.

"May as well," said Cora, and jumped in, giving no thought to the tightness of the space.

It was narrow, but not too narrow for her to fit, and she began to slide at once, gathering speed even before the smaller dinosaur landed against her back, pressing her down at a faster pace. Cora kept her legs straight and her hands pressed against her sides, thinking compressed thoughts. It was like a waterslide with no water. The wood was slick around her, worn smooth by wind and water and, she presumed, past escapes of this nature; she hit no obstacles as she slid down, and was going so fast, it took her already-labored breath away by the time she shot out the other end, landing in a patch of those towering ferns with a thump.

"Oh thank God, Cora," said Kade, hurrying to help her up. "I thought we'd lost you."

"You're the one who left me behind," she said, blinking against the light as she took his hand. Everything was blurry after the long fall through the dark.

"I knew you were holding back to pace me, and when Godzilla popped up, guess I just panicked. You're all right? You're not hurt anywhere?"

"I don't think I am." Cora pushed herself to her feet, plucking a fern frond out of her hair. "I think I'll skip my run tomorrow."

"I think you're entitled."

Cora looked around. All of them had apparently made it down the slide relatively unscathed; Emily had a scrape on one elbow and Sumi's nose was bleeding, but that was the extent of their visible injuries. The feathered dinosaurs were gathered around Stephanie once again, crooning and creeling as she stroked their heads and spoke to them in a voice too low to carry.

"She looks really happy here," she said.

Kade followed her gaze. "Isn't that the point? You or I wouldn't be, and so we were never offered a door that led here."

"But will she *always* be happy in a world with no other people, and no one to take care of her if she hurts herself or gets sick?"

"Maybe. Maybe not. Will any of us always be happy any-where? I was sad plenty in Prism, even when I still thought I belonged there. From the things you've told me about the Trenches, you were sad there, too. Remember?"

Cora hesitated. "I wasn't always bubbling over with joy, no," she said, after a moment to consider. "I saw people die. I killed people. They were monsters and they were trying to destroy us, but they were still people until they weren't anymore. I did terrible things for excellent reasons, and I'd do them all again if I had the chance. But I wasn't *always* happy. I also wasn't alone, or in a place where no one could take care of me."

"That's the second time you've said that," he said. "What makes you think she doesn't have people who'll take care of her? Those dinosaurs are clearly pretty smart, and she can communicate with them, even if she's not using words we understand. Do you really think they'll run off and leave her to die if she breaks her leg or something?"

"No."

"As for alone . . . people are social, as a rule. But there's no one way to be a social animal. She's not alone. And even if she were, we couldn't force her to leave with us. The dinosaurs would never allow it."

"They do have an awful lot of teeth," said Cora.

Antsy walked toward them, Hudson riding on her shoulder. "Hudson can fly up and scout for the big predators; his coloration is enough like the juvenile form of the local flying predators that they leave him alone, and we're too big for them to try to take. Plus apparently, they've taken a few bites out of Stephanie, and they didn't like the way she tasted."

"Mammals aren't a thing here yet," said Stephanie, walking toward the forming cluster with two of her "family members" pacing alongside her, heads bobbing and lips relaxed. They looked friendly, when they weren't snarling. "So we don't taste like food. That's fine when you're dealing with bugs or little dinos, not so fine when you're dealing with the big guys or the venomous ones. Big guys chew you up and spit you out, doesn't make you any less dead. Venomous ones let go fast; again, doesn't make you any less dead."

"Huh," said Kade, shooting a quelling look at Cora. She

shook her head and made a zipping motion across her lips. "Well, we're just glad you're happy here."

"Never been happier," said Stephanie. "I was never a 'people person.' I can get along with them pretty well, but they made fun of my hair and my skin, called me all sorts of names, and you know, anything can be an insult if you shape it the right way before you throw it. 'Albino' isn't an insult, but they turned it into one, every single day."

Cora blinked. "But your eyes—"

"Albinism in humans doesn't always mean pink eyes. We can have blue eyes, even brown, depending on how much pigment we've got. Try telling that to middle school kids. I have to stay out of the sun as much as possible, which hey, now I live with a colony of feathered dinosaurs under the canopy of a massive rainforest. There are clouds in the sky like, *all* the time. I get infections more easily than a lot of people do, but most of the bugs that have figured out how to infect and attack mammals won't evolve for a *whole* lot of years. This is where I belong. This is where I want to be. And if I get eaten by a big lizard who doesn't realize that my proteins will give it a tummy ache, well, that's the price I've got to pay."

"I never thought of it like that," said Cora.

"So Hudson can find us a safe path back to where we left the Door, and we can go relieve Christopher before Vineta finds him and shoves him through and we all wind up trapped in the Land of the Lost." Antsy glanced at Stephanie. "No offense."

"None taken. It's nice to have guests, but you're making the family nervous, and you make a lot of noise. I'll be glad to see you go."

"I found a fruit that tries to run away when you touch it!" chirped Sumi. "Can I have one for a pet?"

Kade glanced to Stephanie, who was shaking her head and making violent "no" gestures. "I don't think that's a good idea, Sumi. Come on, let's get moving."

Sumi sulked but came to join the others.

"Where's Emily?" asked Antsy, looking around. When she abruptly stopped and made a small gasping sound, the others turned to see what she was looking at.

Emily was dancing with one of the dinosaurs.

The steps were improvised, but they matched each other swoop for swoop and spin for spin, hair and feathers flying. It was beautiful and strange and something they could never have seen anywhere else, not if they had lived for a thousand years.

One of the other dinosaurs chirped, and Emily's partner stopped, head ducked in what looked like a strange combination of embarrassment and regret. It nudged Emily's cheek with the tip of its muzzle, then ran back to join the rest of the flock, allowing itself to be preened back into glossy sleekness. Emily walked over to the group.

"Dance is a universal language," she said, in answer to their questioning looks. "He seemed to want to talk to me, so we did."

"What did you talk about?" asked Antsy.

"Dancing, mostly."

Hudson launched himself into the air with a frantic flurry of black-and-white wings, rapidly gaining altitude and circling high overhead for a moment before gliding back down and saying, "Follow me."

"Directions from birds and running away from dinosaurs;

this is the most normal day I've had in forever," said Sumi brightly. She waved to Stephanie. "Glad we got to see you again, glad the dinosaurs didn't eat you, glad you're not coming with us."

Stephanie waved back. "Be careful out there. There's a lot of things around here that don't realize you're not food."

"What a fun way to say goodbye," said Cora, as they began walking after Antsy. "Not ominous at all. Nothing about this is disturbing. I'm having a wonderful time."

"Aw, c'mon." Kade elbowed her lightly in the side. "You know you're enjoying this. A wild adventure, a quest—"

"Don't the school rules say no quests?"

"Has that actually stopped us at any point?"

Cora sighed. "No. But I keep hoping it will."

"You'd rather sit around being bored all the time?"

"I'm rooming with *Sumi*. I'm never bored." Cora linked her hands behind her head, looking up at the sky as they walked. Hudson flew loops overhead, unhurried, easily keeping pace with the slower bipeds below him. "I was talking to Emily earlier, about why she didn't want Antsy to find her door; she wanted her door to come to her, when it thought she was sure enough. And I realized, I want the same thing."

"Oh?"

"Yeah. Is that silly? Maybe. I don't know. Is it falling into that awful pattern of self-denial, where I have to be good enough to earn the treat I've promised myself before I'm allowed to have it? I think there's a good chance. Never eat dessert before dinner, or you're being naughty."

"I don't think I've ever seen Sumi eat anything *but* dessert," said Kade.

"From the things she's said about her childhood, she got all her dinners out of the way a long time before she went to Confection, and now it's dessert all the time, forever. But anyway. I worried about my parents missing me the first time I was in the Trenches. I worried about how much it must be hurting them, not knowing where I was, afraid they'd lost me. I worried about what the other kids at school would think. I worried about a lot of things. I think that's why I wasn't sure enough. That's the trick, really. We ask, again and again, why the doors take kids, and I think it's a combination of things—kids are more flexible, they adjust better to things like 'Oh hey, I'm a mermaid now' or 'Oh hey, that's a dinosaur,' or 'Oh hey, the world is made of candy.' They don't argue that something can't exist when it's looking them right in the eye."

"That's one thing. You said it was a combination."

"Oh. Yeah. I think it's easy for adults to assume kids have less to lose, but they don't, not really. It's just that the things we have haven't been around as long, and that means they're not guaranteed to stay. If you're not sure because you want to eat your grandmother's pie one more time, and you come back and she's gone, well, now you were unsure for nothing. Your favorite dolly may be a good enough reason to want to go home, but there's a pretty solid chance your parents threw her out while you were on the other side of the rainbow, and she's gone for good. And I think kids know that. Kids know the things they love weren't here yesterday, and they're smart enough to see how that can easily mean those things won't be there tomorrow."

"Huh," said Kade. "I always thought kids had less to lose."

"Did you, when Prism took you? Or did you miss the things you didn't have anymore?"

"My folks used to ship me off to the cousins every summer, said it was good for me, would build character, and Daddy thought I needed character. Helped that my cousins were all girls—Jenny was even a horse girl—and all my friends in the neighborhood were boys. So I was already used to having the things I cared about taken away whether or not I said I was all right with it."

"That's *terrible*."

"That's why I was always sure. They didn't boot me because my faith wavered. They did it because I wasn't who they wanted me to be, and I'm not forgiving them for that."

"I just . . . One day, I realized I didn't remember what bread tasted like anymore. Dry bread, eaten in the air, not soaked through and swept overboard during a storm. And remembering bread made me remember my mother, and that I loved her, and then I felt bad for needing bread to remind me she existed." Cora shrugged. "I guess I lost conviction over a hug and a sandwich."

"More's been lost for less, Cora. Do you still want those things?"

"Bread wasn't anything like I remembered it being. And I do love my mother, but she stopped calling a few months after I went to school—said it was too hard for her. I think she just can't handle the fact that I'm not going to be the kid she wanted me to be. It was always hard on her, when I didn't fit her ideas of the perfect, pretty, petite little daughter."

"And that's why you won't ask Antsy to find your door?"

"Yeah." Cora lowered her eyes, looking at him. "My parents didn't choose me after I went and got myself lost. I didn't choose them, either. I want the Trenches to choose me. I want them to take me home because they know it's where I'm supposed to be. If I have to wait a long, long time for that to happen, so be it. Eleanor's proof that the doors don't have deadlines."

Their flight from the big predator had taken them deeper into the jungle than they'd realized at the time, but they were walking out of it now, holes appearing in the canopy overhead to let the primordial sunlight come slicing through in shafts of buttery, oxygen-rich light. Little insects danced there, glorying in their world and their time, and Kade wondered abstractly if they would ever reach a point in their development where they had thoughts and dreams and things to run away from. Were there doors for things he'd never recognize as human? Did butterflies sometimes find themselves swept away to worlds where the flowers were sweeter, or stranger, or sang them sad flower songs?

That was a question without an answer, and so he just nodded, shot Cora an encouraging smile, and said, "Hope's still Sumi's least favorite word there is, but you're not Sumi, and I hope you find your door one day. I hope that when the time comes, we'll be able to say goodbye."

Cora knew he hadn't been able to say goodbye to Nancy, and so she only nodded, and kept walking.

13 THE LONG WAIT

CHRISTOPHER FELT AS IF he'd been sitting with his back against the shelf of other people's lost possessions forever. His butt had certainly been given plenty of time to go numb, and the skeletal mice and beetles he'd piped out from under the shelves were no longer gamboling around his feet but moving slowly back and forth, rolling dust bunnies out from under the shelves and dredging crumbs out of the cracks in the floor. Watching them was something to do, at least, and so he kept them awake and moving.

Beetles didn't have bones, but they had chitin, and whatever magic his flute possessed seemed to work on it just fine. He didn't think about it too hard. Better to stay alert and listen for signs that Vineta or Yulia was looking for him. He wasn't sure what sort of threat a little girl or an old woman could present, but he'd long since learned that appearances could be deceiving, especially when trying to figure out how dangerous something was. The Skeleton Girl had seemed like a living nightmare the first time he'd seen her, all long bones walking around without anything to hold her up, painted skull gleaming in the honeyed Mariposa sun. But by the time he'd been whisked away, back into the alley behind the hospital he'd run from, the smell of rot and disinfectant in the air, she'd been the most beautiful woman he had ever seen. Seraphina, now . . . she couldn't affect him with her pearlized glory, but he could still recognize that she was the kind of beautiful that had no reason to exist. She was loveliness turned lethal, and she didn't belong to their world anymore.

None of them did, not really. Some of them could adjust to reentry, like Kade, or Nichole, who insisted that she was happier with a license to help kids like she'd been than she could ever have been in the world on the other side of her door—although she never gave details about it, not the way that Lundy had. It was like for her, adjusting meant putting every piece of where she'd gone in a box and setting it safely on a shelf, where it could be admired from a distance but couldn't touch her.

Christopher didn't feel like that. He woke up every morning missing his Skeleton Girl, and he remained immune to things like Seraphina's charms for the same reason he would have been unaffected by the world's most breathtaking vista or most beautiful bird: he didn't want to be with any woman who needed to cloak herself in flesh and blood. Or at least that was why he assumed he was immune. He didn't honestly know. No one did. Maybe it was something about his connection to the dead, or maybe he was just lucky. Magic was funny that way.

If he didn't find his door again, he sometimes thought he'd wind up having a fabulous career as a very strange serial killer, stripping every woman whose voice he found even remotely attractive down to the bone in his pursuit of his lost love. He didn't *want* that future, didn't think he'd done anything to deserve it, but it was one of the only outcomes he could see of being returned to his family, with their endless pressure to find someone, some "real girl" who existed in their world, fall in love, and do the things they expected of an adult.

Christopher tilted his head back, looking at the distant

ceiling. Even the rafters had been pressed into use, support-
ing hanging taxidermy and model aircraft, as well as what
looked like dangerously precarious free-hanging shelves, sup-
ported by a few loops of rope or chain and, one hoped, a lot
of engineering skill.

As he was staring at the shelf above him, distantly wondering whether it was going to come crashing down and answer the question of whether he was even going to return
to Mariposa once and for all, he heard voices drifting from
the other side of the still-propped door. He sat up at once,
eyes snapping to the opening. There had been a lot of sounds
since the others left—the whistling of the wind, the warble of
something that sounded almost but not quite like a bird, and
the furious roaring of something big enough to eat the world.
But there had been no voices. Whatever kind of world was
out there, he didn't think it had a lot of people in it.

The voices got closer—not close enough for him to make
out words but close enough for him to make out tones, and
he bounced to his feet, pulling the door the rest of the way
open as he watched his friends make their way through the
sea of ferns toward the door.

"Oh, good," called Antsy, audibly relieved. "You kept it
open."

There was a large black-and-white bird riding on her
shoulder. For some reason, it was wearing glasses. That didn't
seem to be bothering any of the rest of them, and so Christopher decided that it wasn't going to bother him, either.

"No one came this way while I was waiting," he said. "But
I was starting to get really bored. You guys okay?"

There was something that looked like blood on Sumi's lips
and chin, and Kade was limping. Cora nodded.

"We got sort of chased by something out of a Godzilla movie, but we found Hudson and we didn't get eaten, so I guess we can call this trip a success. And we ran into one of our old roommates from Whitethorn."

Christopher blinked. "This day has been so weird, that doesn't even seem strange at this point. Infinite worlds out there, filled with infinite versions of reality, so of course you'd wind up in one where a former classmate had taken refuge. Why wouldn't you?"

"We don't believe all possible worlds connect to any one Nexus," said Hudson primly, as Antsy stepped through the doorway and back into the Store. Taking a deep breath, he ruffled his feathers, puffing them out in obvious pleasure. "Oh, *there's* the smell of home. This is as it's meant to be, books and dust and other people's possessions." For all his delight, he remained firmly on Antsy's shoulder.

"Meaning what?" asked Christopher.

"Meaning that every Nexus—this Store and your Earth, assuming you all come from the same original world as Antsy—has perhaps two or three hundred worlds close enough to form a stable connection, and won't reach anything farther away than that. Much as I hate to admit that we have limitations, I'm sure there are worlds accessible from Earth that cannot be reached from here, and very likely vice versa. But where are my manners? I'm Hudson."

The bird bowed, spreading his wings in a gesture very much like a human trying to make a good impression might spread his arms. His glasses, which were joined together at the back of his head, didn't budge. Bobbing back to an upright position, he continued. "I'm one of the magpies native to this world. We were here before anything else, when we were just the junkshop Nexus of this corner of reality. We didn't build the Store, but we helped as best we could, and we've always given our support to the shopkeepers."

"So you're on Vineta's side?" asked Sumi, nudging Antsy aside to let the others through the door. "I don't like her. She's a mean lady."

"I was, once." Hudson's wings drooped. "We stopped telling the new arrivals what the doors would cost them five keepers ago. The keeper we had then said that knowing had only caused him pain, that he wished we'd allowed him to spend his life in innocence, instead of turning it into something he had to hoard, and he demanded we let the next keepers come and go in innocence and ignorance. We agreed, because we've always allowed the keepers to set the rules of the Store itself. They stock the shelves and change the lightbulbs, and they live out their whole lives in our world, separated from their own. Why shouldn't we allow them a little autonomy, when it relates to their own kind and isn't hurting anyone?

"But Elodina, the first shopkeeper, the one who called this place into being with blood and sweat and *needing,* began to stir in her long slumber, pulling strength from the Store itself. And then she began to appear to the keepers. Antoinette was the third to hear her message, and the first to take it to heart."

He bowed his head again, this time in regret. "Antoinette told us we had robbed her, that by lying to her, we had hurt her as much as the people she ran from. This is meant to be a sanctuary. A place where travelers can be safe, for as long as they need to be. For some, aging faster is a blessing, and there have been keepers who returned to their worlds of origin, able to go back once they felt confident that no one would be able to recognize them. For others, it's a curse. But after Antoinette told us we were going to do things differently, the Store saw fit to send her home, and Vineta said that proved she was wrong, and we had been doing things correctly for all these years. She made me promise not to tell the next apprentice what the costs were, but she forgot that a new promise doesn't come before an older one, and I had already promised Antoinette I'd tell."

He launched himself from Antsy's shoulder then, flying to a nearby shelf and landing on a tree-shaped bookend before he turned to face her. "I taught her the rhyme of keepers. The counting rhyme that shows how fast they come and go. She thought it was a funny little song. I told her of Elodina. She said it was sad, and didn't care. I kept trying, and she kept refusing to listen. Then Vineta caught us, and said the Store had no need of magpies, not with a keeper and an apprentice. She told Yulia all birds were liars, and she put me in a cage and had the child open a Door so they could toss me away. I thought I would never be home again. I thought I was lost forever."

"Now you know how I feel," said Antsy. "How could the Store just throw me out like that? It took my entire childhood!"

"You're assuming intent," said Hudson. He cocked his head, looking at her gravely. "There is no intent. The Doors can see who suits a world, and if that person doesn't suit the one they're in, they can come and offer an alternative. But it's only that—an alternative. Any uncertainty, any belief that they might be better off where they were, and the Doors will send them back again. Did you waver, at all?"

"I was angry!" said Antsy. "You *stole* from me! You didn't *listen*!"

"And you wanted, if only for a moment, to go back to where things were simple, and you wouldn't have to make decisions or be responsible for convincing others to keep their words to you," said Hudson. "You weren't sure."

"I'm sure *now*," said Antsy.

"Good. Then you'll stay, and be our keeper, and Vineta will be reminded that all keepers are here at the sufferance of the birds who guide them."

Christopher ran his fingers nervously along the length of his flute, feeling the familiar indentations like a lifeline. "Are you saying we have to kill her?"

"What? No!" Hudson sounded appropriately horrified by the idea. "No, we'll just send her back where she came from. Her services are no longer needed."

Dimly, Antsy remembered Vineta's explanation of her own origins. Fifteen and running from an arranged marriage. She'd never said anything else about the world she came from, never given it a name or refused to walk through one of the Doors Antsy opened because it might lead her back to a place that had long since ceased to be home.

"That's cruel," she said, horrified. "She was only fifteen when she ran away from there. She's an old woman now. She won't know anyone, or how anything is done, and it's not like she can go back to her family."

"We offered her a nest and she abused it," said Hudson. "We might have been able to forgive the lying; she'll die long before Yulia is used up, and I could have kept my promise to you once she was gone. But as soon as Vineta put me in a cage and threw me out to die, she lost the right to expect kindness from our kind. All keepers serve on the behalf of the shop, and not the other way around."

Antsy nodded slowly. The logic was undeniable, if harsh.

"So we confront her," she said.

"No," said Hudson. "You confront her. I will gather the mischief, and we'll pass our own judgment."

Then he flew away, high into the rafters, vanishing in the shadows. The cluster of out of place teens looked at one another.

"When I first got here, Vineta told me that she couldn't open Doors anymore," said Antsy. "She said they stopped working for her. It's pretty clear that wasn't true—she just ran out of time she didn't need to keep herself alive. What if we throw her out and she can find the Doors outside the Store the same way I can? What if she just comes back?"

"Then you throw her out again," said Kade.

Antsy looked at him, miserable. "I don't know if I can push an old woman out of her home over and over again, even after she hurt me the way she did. She didn't push *me* out when we disagreed. She let my own uncertainty do it for me."

"It took us two doors to get here," said Cora. "Do you think that was about the normal number, or was that a short route?"

Antsy hesitated. "The Doors . . . they're not clever. They have a function, and they do it. I don't know why the system exists, or why the Doors work the way they do, but it does, and so do they. I do like to think, though, that since they're a sort of . . . an immune system for making worlds better? That maybe they can act a little bit intentionally when they get something really wrong. So that feels like it was a short route. Like they were putting the Doors that would get us here the fastest where I could find them."

"So say it's normally four doors, not two," said Cora. "She'll be traveling alone, and she's *very* old. Even assuming she started hunting for doors immediately, I don't think you'd have to worry about her coming back here more than once."

"I wish I didn't have to worry about it at all."

"Well, it's not going to happen just because we stand around here talking about how awful it's going to be," said Sumi, picking up a croquet mallet from where it leaned against a nearby shelf. She gave it an experimental swing before smacking it against her open palm in punctuation, then slung it over her shoulder and grinned at the group, feral as always. "Let's go serve an eviction notice."

"You know you're terrifying, right?" asked Emily, walking close to Sumi as the group started moving. "It's really important to me that you know you're terrifying. Stephanie lives with dinosaurs, Christopher sings to skeletons, and I used to dance with scarecrows around a bonfire that never burned down, no matter how long the night lasted, and I still say you're the terrifying one."

Sumi favored her with a beatific grin. "I am, and it's great, and I'm still a hero with her best world-saving days ahead of her, so I plan to enjoy it for just as long as I can. I'm not as terrifying in Confection."

Emily glanced to the others, seeking some confirmation of this statement, and Kade nodded. "She's right," he said. "Bunch of us went there to bring Sumi back from the dead in the first place—and that was what kicked off this whole run of quests—and that world's pretty and sugar-sweet and dangerous as hell. I'd rather go back to the Moors."

Cora shuddered.

"Is this a quest?" asked Antsy.

"We're worlds away from home with no way back unless you help us, trying to take your Store back from a woman who lies to and steals from children, and puts intelligent birds in cages so she can feed them to whatever comes along," said Kade. "Yeah, this is a quest. Whether or not we want it to be, this is a quest. And if we fail, we may not be able to find a way back to the school."

"I'll get you back unless Vineta kills me," said Antsy. "I'm staying here, but I'll get you back."

"Don't make promises until you're certain you can keep them," chirped Sumi, and that was somehow the truest and the most terrifying thing anyone had said that day, so they walked on in silence, letting those words linger in the air a little longer.

The Store played no tricks with distance this time, and they hadn't been walking for very long when they rounded a corner and saw the counter, currently unoccupied, with the curtained room beyond it. Antsy didn't bother ringing the bell. She went straight to the little waist-high door off to the side, unhooked it, and stepped through, pausing to relatch it before turning to the others.

"Staff only, and the Store knows how to enforce it," she said. "I'll be right back."

"Wait—are you currently staff?" asked Cora.

Antsy shrugged. "I'll be right back," she repeated, and ducked through the curtain, into the hidden room beyond.

She didn't reemerge. Cora started to step toward the little swinging door, and stopped when Kade's hand landed on her shoulder, tugging her back.

"Wait," he said. "Give her time."

"But that woman could come back at any second—"

And as if Cora's words had been some sort of invocation, a door that had been standing propped open in a nearby aisle swung open and Vineta stepped through, a wicker shopping basket slung over one arm, greenery spilling out over the sides, and a paper bag that smelled of pastry in her hand. Yulia was close behind her, lugging her own basket, which looked substantially heavier and filled with cheese, apples, and onions. No meat, though.

Given Kade's guesses about her origins, he wasn't surprised. Jill had always been an enthusiastic eater of flesh, the bloodier the better, while Jack, for all her squeamishness, had refused to veer from a vegetarian diet until after she'd been allowed to visit the local farm Eleanor bought their meat from. Only knowing for sure that the bacon came from a pig rather than a person had allowed her to relax and stop watching the other students eat with the wary guardedness of someone who had fallen into an entire colony of cannibals. Yulia's meatless basket was not remarkable.

Judging by the way Vineta stumbled and stopped, their presence was. And that was even without taking into account Sumi, who was now sitting on the counter and smacking her croquet mallet into the palm of her hand, over and over again, making a rhythmic slapping sound.

"You left," accused Vineta.

"We didn't close the door behind us," said Emily. "We were going to find something, and once we found it, we came back."

Vineta glanced around, eyes widening in apparent alarm. "Is he *here*?" she asked.

"Hudson? No. He went to take care of something," said Cora. "We're here, though, and we're going to have a little chat with you about adults who hurt kids on purpose."

"You would come and threaten an old woman in her home?" asked Vineta. "Nasty children. Wicked children. How dare you behave in such a manner?"

"How dare *you* think that just because you were hurt, it's okay to keep hurting others? That just because you had to pay, no one ever gets to change the system?" Kade shook his head. "It doesn't have to work like that."

"I'm not hurting anyone."

"Aren't you?"

Yulia was glancing uncertainly between Vineta and Kade. Emily crouched down and beckoned the girl toward her, taking the basket out of her hands with a soothing murmur and setting it on the floor.

"It's okay, it's okay," she said. "No one's going to hurt you anymore."

"I don't want to leave," said Yulia. "Please, don't make me leave. The vampires are waiting for me to come back to where I used to live, and if they catch me, they'll swallow me up and I'll be gone forever."

"We're not going to make you leave," said Emily.

"Then the harm you say I'm doing continues," said Vineta. "She can't stay here if she doesn't work, and the people who live in the shop can't get by without the Doors. Antoinette accuses me of liking my little treats and luxuries, and maybe that's so—maybe sometimes I've gotten a little greedy and brought back more than was absolutely needed in the moment. But we need food and we need drink and we need medicine, and those are things that aren't often lost when there's still virtue left in them. We have to be able to travel."

"We still can," said Antsy, emerging from behind the curtain at last. "When it's necessary, we still can. There's a difference between a Door a week and ten Doors in a day. People shouldn't be used up for the sake of novelty and not needing to decide today what tomorrow's dinner is going to be. The

Store needs keepers, and the keepers need Doors to do our job. That doesn't mean we let people open them willy-nilly without knowing the price."

"What were you going to do with those days, Antoinette? How were you going to spend them that was so much better than seeing wonders and touching the whole universe? I didn't steal anything you weren't happy to give away."

Antsy scowled. "You know, when I was here and worked for you, I could never tell where the Door I was about to open would lead. And now I can. They even *look* different to me than they used to. They always looked like they were a part of the Store before, part of *this* world, and now when I look at them, they look like they belong to the worlds they lead *to*. Leaving and being sure enough that I wanted to come back that I started really *looking* did that for me. Maybe it could have done it for any of us. Let us stay until we're uncertain, but make sure we know how much time we're losing, so we realize that time is short, and we need to be uncertain *now* if we're going to do it at all. Then, when we leave and need to come back, we can find our way."

"You can't live a life on 'maybe'," scoffed Vineta.

"Why not? Everyone else does." Antsy looked to Yulia. "I won't make you leave. You ran away for a reason, and you deserve to be safe while you're growing up. But you also deserve to decide how fast that happens."

"And what about me?" asked Vineta. "Am I to stand idly by as you destroy everything I've spent my life working for?"

"No," said Antsy sadly. "Much worse than that."

And the light dimmed around them as the distant windows were blacked out by the widespread wings of furious birds.

14 MAGPIES HAVE LONG MEMORIES

VINETA LOOKED UP IN alarm, eyes going wide and face going whey-white and sickly. She dropped her basket, staggering backward.

"This isn't right," she said. "I've served long and well! I've been shopkeeper through *three* mewling assistants! No one else, not even Elodina, has ever managed to stay for *three*! You need me! I'm the one who knows how it all works, and you *need* me!"

"The people who own this world have a right to have a say in how it's used, and you took that away from them," said Antsy.

"Bad birds," gasped Yulia, burying her face against Emily's arm.

"They know we're not *with* her, right?" asked Christopher, as an aside to Cora.

Overhead, glass broke with a shattering crack.

Cora grimaced. "I don't know," she said.

"It's all right," said Antsy. "Hudson will have told them who's on their side and who's not."

She turned her attention back to Vineta, and her expression was terrible and cold.

"If you run now, you might find a Door," said Antsy, as the birds poured in above her head like a furious cloud, the sound of their wings and cries filling the air. "You won't know where it goes, but it's probably better than being driven through a Door you didn't choose."

"How *dare* you?" gasped Vineta.

"How dare *you*?" countered Antsy, much more calmly, as the magpies began to descend.

Hudson was the first to land, touching down delicately on his waiting perch. He cocked his head, light reflecting from his glasses. "Vineta, the Mischief of Magpies who rule the Land Where the Lost Things Go has decided that your services will no longer be required. You may now vacate our property. I would suggest you do so quickly."

More and more magpies were landing. Some, like Hudson, wore glasses; others had monocles, or cuffs on their legs, or fancy little hats. The majority were unclothed, and looked like any other magpie, anywhere. All their eyes were fixed on Vineta, hard and furious and making it all but impossible to ignore how sharp their beaks were, how pointed their talons.

Vineta turned and ran, faster than any of them would have expected a woman her age to move, and the magpies followed.

Sumi slid off the counter, looking only faintly disappointed that she hadn't been given an excuse to start breaking bones with a croquet mallet. "Birds are scary," she said.

None of them could disagree.

Antsy walked over where Yulia still pressed her face into Emily's arm, crouching down. "Hello," she said.

Yulia peeked at her. "'lo," she replied.

"So I'm going to be running things here for a little while, with the help of the magpies."

"Mostly me!" said Hudson.

Antsy smiled. "Mostly Hudson. I know you don't want to go back to the world you came from, and I won't make you, but you still have a choice."

"A choice?" sniffled Yulia, finally turning to face Antsy altogether.

"Everyone gets choices," said Antsy firmly. "My friends are going back to the school they all attend, and you could go with them. The woman who owns it is kind to kids like us, she'll make sure you're safe and taken care of, and have everything you need. Or you can stay here, but if you do, you have to do as you're told, even if you don't always like it."

"You won't hurt me?"

"Never intentionally," said Antsy. "There will still be Doors to open, if you stay here, but we'll open them at a pace you feel comfortable with, and you'll have time between them to grow up at the speed you should. We'll figure it out together."

"And you know where the Doors go? So I won't accidentally open one that leads to where I came from?"

"Yes."

"But I *could* go back, someday, if I wanted."

"Yes," said Antsy again.

Yulia took a deep breath as she pulled away from Emily, straightening. "I'm going to stay here," she said. "With you. I'll help keep the shelves stocked and make sure the customers find what they need, and I'll be happy, because there aren't any vampires."

The magpies that hadn't gone after Vineta cawed their approval of the plan, voices ringing from the rafters.

Antsy nodded. "All right. And if you ever change your mind, we can find you someplace else to be." She turned to the others. "The same offer's open to all of you," she said. "If any of you want to stay here, with me, you can. Or I can send you back to the school, or I can send you . . ."

"Home," said Emily, and the longing in her voice was an agony. "School for me, please. Harvest will call me when it feels I'm sure enough."

"Never going back," said Kade. "School."

"I *know* I'm going home, and I don't need to cut the line," said Sumi.

"The school is not going to be okay if we don't figure out how we're dealing with Seraphina. Right now, they need me, and I'd always feel bad for leaving them in the lurch," said Christopher.

They looked to Cora, who took a deep, shaking breath.

"I'm . . . torn," she admitted. "I want to go back to the school. I don't want to let those mean girls think they ran me off. But I want to go home, more than anything. I think, though, that as long as I *can* be torn, I'm not sure enough. I'll go back to school."

"All of you?" asked Antsy.

They nodded.

"All right," she said. "The door you need is this way. Only one, this time."

"I'll open it," said Sumi.

"I won't argue," said Antsy, and laughed. "This all feels so grown-up, when I'm angry because they didn't let me be a kid when I was supposed to."

"I don't think we get second chances with our own injuries," said Sumi. "All we can really do is try to clean up all the broken glass before someone else gets there."

Antsy nodded, and on they walked until they reached the front door of the school. It was plain, weathered and familiar, and as welcoming as anything. Antsy gestured for Sumi to take the knob. Sumi reached out to do so . . . and then hesitated, glancing at Kade.

"You know," she said, "I was dead for a while."

"You never stop reminding us," said Christopher dryly.

"So I'm younger than I'm supposed to be, and maybe that's part of why the timeline isn't unsnarling enough to make it feel like the right time to get back to Ponder and the war. Maybe I just need to be a little older."

Kade blinked. "Sumi, you're not saying—"

"Not forever," said Sumi. "Just until I catch up. It shouldn't take all that long, with all these doors. I need to get you alone. We need to have a little talk, you and me, but not when there's anyone else around, and not when we're already in the middle of a quest that wants to be finished before we get distracted. So you wait for me, okay? As soon as I'm old enough, I'll come back to school so we can talk and the door to Confection can find me."

"You little weirdo," said Kade, and hugged her, almost knocking the croquet mallet out of her hands. Sumi laughed and hugged him back, while Emily and Antsy exchanged confused looks and Cora and Christopher looked resigned.

"What's happening?" asked Emily.

"I'm going to stay here and help with the transition," said Sumi. "And if any mean ladies who lie to kids try to crawl out of the woodwork, I'll make sure they leave without doing any more damage."

"But you're coming back, right?"

"As soon as I catch up to myself, solemn swear," said Sumi, and opened the door on the entry hall of the school, smiling brightly at the rest of them as she did. "Maybe I'll even get that nifty trick Antsy can do, empty the place out. Now get out of here before we change our minds."

"Jerk," said Kade, and stepped through.

"Thank you," said Emily, following.

"You *better* come back," said Christopher, before he left.

Cora hesitated.

"It's not too late," said Antsy.

"I'm still not sure," said Cora. "You're a jerk but I love you, Sumi. I won't touch any of your stuff before you get back."

"You can touch the perishables, or they'll perish," said Sumi, and watched as Cora stepped through. Then she let go.

The door swung shut, and disappeared.

EPILOGUE
DEPARTURES

THREE MONTHS WITHOUT SUMI basically meant three months of peace. No quests had cropped up, no chaos had erupted, and only two new students had arrived, both of whom Kade had assessed as coming from Logical worlds, one Wicked, one Virtuous, and who had merged easily into the student body. Angela and Seraphina had been placed on probation as a consequence of their actions: they were currently banned from all extracurricular activities, required to attend nightly counseling with Nichole, and Christopher was working with Seraphina to find ways to reduce her impact on the people around her, and possibly live a more normal life.

Eleanor hadn't wanted to expel either girl on a first offense, and Kade thought Antsy would have approved of that. She had given Vineta a chance to do better, after all; why shouldn't Eleanor give Angela and Seraphina the same?

Using the information gained on their brief travels, Kade had finally managed to persuade Eleanor to leave classifying the worlds to him, citing her tendency to see Nonsense where none existed as detrimental, and to everyone's surprised delight, she'd agreed. He was still reassessing the rest of the student body, resulting in several roommate swaps and substantially fewer arguments. Sometimes he even got time to himself.

That was what led to him being out jogging with Cora in the early afternoon, the two of them circling the turtle pond.

"I still hate this," he wheezed.

"I know," she said, much less breathlessly. "But if we ever need to run away from dinosaurs again, you'll be so glad you did." She sped up to get ahead of him and turned to run backward so she could watch his face.

"You're a sadist," he accused, without heat.

"Maybe," she said brightly. "Need a break?"

"Lord, *please*," he said.

Laughing, she slowed to a stop, putting her hands at the small of her back and stretching as she turned to look out across the turtle pond.

"Can this really be enough?" she asked.

"What do you mean?"

"We saw *magic*. We fought *armies*. This—school, class, phys ed, waiting to graduate and figure out what happens next—can it really be enough?"

"It is for me," said Kade.

"Not for me," said Cora. "I know we're supposed to get over it, but I can't. I want to go home."

"Then go home," said a voice behind them, accompanied by the sound of a closing door. "You make it sound like it's hard or something."

"Sumi!" exclaimed Kade, whirling around to face her.

Explaining Sumi's absence had been the hardest part of coming back. Antsy had blown in with the wind and mostly kept to herself; it didn't surprise anyone when she'd blown out the same way. Sumi, though . . . Sumi was a fixture. Everyone knew she'd leave them someday, but someday was never supposed to be right *now*.

Cora didn't turn.

Sumi grinned at Kade. "Miss me?" she asked.

"Oh you *brat*!" he said, and lunged toward her, grabbing

her around the middle and lifting her off the ground as he spun her around. Sumi squealed, totally delighted.

"Bad, *bad* man," she scolded, lightly hitting his shoulder. "Put me down."

"Let me look at you!" Kade set her on her feet and took a step back.

Sumi spread her arms and did a little turn, showing off her patchwork vest and trousers. Dozens of cheap glass-bead necklaces hung around her neck, and more beads were anchored in her hair, worn as always in two messy pigtails. It was hard for a teen looking at a teen to tell the subtle gradations in age, but she looked about a year older—very close to the amount of time she'd been dead.

"I caught up," she said, happily.

"Yes, you did," he agreed. "Welcome home."

"Kade?"

Cora's voice was soft, almost shaking. He looked over his shoulder. She was still standing frozen, staring at the turtle pond.

"What is it, mermaid?" asked Sumi. "I missed you, too. Nice to have such an enthusiastic greeting."

Cora didn't reply or shift her gaze, just made a soft choking sound.

The two of them moved to flank her, looking down at the water. After a moment's silence, Kade said, "Whatever you're looking at—"

"We can't see it," said Sumi, cutting him off. "But is it there?"

Cora nodded, raising one hand to press against her mouth, tears shining in her eyes.

"Are you sure?" asked Kade, then winced, realizing what he'd said. "Aw, hell, Cora, I didn't mean—"

"I'm sure," she said. "I'm really, truly sure. It's there, and it's beautiful, and it's been waiting for me."

She dropped her hand and reached for his, still not looking away. It was as if she were afraid that even glancing at him for a second would turn the truth into a mirage, like this was all too fragile to be trusted.

"I told you I'd try to make it so we had time," she said, voice small.

And Kade nodded. "You did."

"Goodbye, Kade."

"Goodbye, Cora. And . . . thank you."

Cora pulled her hand out of his and stepped forward, into the turtle pond, into the wild, deep wetness, through a door that only she could see. There was no splash. The ripples on the water were the only sign that she had ever been there at all. Kade watched as they spread out to strike the waterweeds and vanish before finally turning away, toward Sumi, who wrapped her arms around him and hugged him close.

"Welcome home," he said again, before he began to cry.